The SKULL & LAUREL

MW00667574

STAFF
Editor-in-Chief: Alex Woodroe
Publisher: Matt Blairstone
Editor: Cameron Howard
Designer: Braulio Tellez
Dose of Dread editor: Alex Ebenstein

Associate editors: j ambrose, Michael Bettendorf, Emma Cole, Kriston T. G. Evenson, Zachary Gillan, Finja Hennicken, Christian M. Ivey, Dany M., Sara S. Messenger, Hazel Zorn

Cover art: WolfSkullJack
Inside art: Samir Sirk Morató

Content Warnings are available at the end of this issue.
Please consult this list for any particular subject matter you may be sensitive to.

Visit our website at www.tenebrouspress.com.
First Printing, October 2024.
The characters and events portrayed in this work are fictitious. Any similarity to real persons, living or dead, is coincidental and not intended by the author.
Print ISBN: 978-1-959790-27-3
eBook ISBN: 978-1-959790-28-0

TABLE OF CONTENTS

Fiction

Nonfiction

Et cetera

Letter from the Editor

THE FIRST ISSUE OF A MAGAZINE ESTABLISHES ITS TONE and what readers can expect in the future. In that sense, I believe this issue successfully conveys what we at *The Skull & Laurel* mean when we talk about New Weird Fiction. Since the stories contained speak for themselves, for my first letter from the editor, I'd like to express my gratitude to those without whom this magazine would not have been possible.

Often overlooked, a magazine's staff can go unrecognized beyond their brief mention on the title page. I'm but one part of a collective effort to bring you the best fiction, so please allow me to duck the spotlight and give them their flowers.

Since we first met, long before I joined the team at Tenebrous Press, Alex Woodroe has been a mentor to me. Editing with her is a dream, and every editorial decision is the result of an ongoing conversation between us. I'm grateful for her continued guidance as I develop as an editor. Matt Blairstone, the other half of 10p's leadership, manages the thousands of tasks required to ensure this magazine gets into your hands. When people at conventions first see the skull and laurel banner, he's always there to meet them, connections that are only made because he travels across the country to be there.

I've been fortunate to work with Braulio Tellez, *The Skull & Laurel's* designer, for the better part of seven years. He's been an indispensable part of every publication I've edited, and more than anyone he is responsible for the look and feel of the magazine. I hope to be his partner in crime for years to come.

The work of Samir Sirk Morató, a returning artist from *Thank You For Joining the Algorithm,* is the final piece that establishes our magazine's identity. Their skillful manipulation of public domain images allows art from the past to live again in the strange new shapes that grace these pages.

I also want to thank Alex Ebenstein for trusting us with his revival of *Dose of Dread,* a flash horror feature that I hope will accompany every issue of *The Skull & Laurel.* Dynamite comes in small packages, and pound for pound his section is sure to pack the biggest punch.

Our associate editor team, lifesavers all, works tirelessly to wrangle the monumental slush pile and give each submission the careful reading it deserves. Their perspectives have been an invaluable asset to the editorial process, granting us insights that simply wouldn't be accessible otherwise. j ambrose, Michael Bettendorf, Emma Cole, Kriston T. G. Evenson, Zachary Gillan, Fi, Christian M. Ivey, Dany M., Sara S. Messenger, and Hazel Zorn; thank each and every one of you.

I'd also like to thank my partner for always supporting me in my endeavors as an editor, even when that means putting up with me spending the small hours hyperfocusing on even smaller details. Her love, respect, and patience are what allow me to stay the course despite life's disruptions.

Finally, I'd like to thank you, the reader holding this magazine. More specifically, I'd like to thank the 420 people whose patronage allowed us to reach nearly double our funding goal for our first year. All remaining funds after fulfilling subscriptions will go toward ensuring the next year of *The Skull & Laurel* is weirder and more wonderful than the first. This security is a privilege that is exceedingly rare in an increasingly turbulent publishing industry — something we are immensely grateful for and won't take for granted.

My hope is that the pages and issues that follow will honor our commitment to publishing genre fiction that is diverse, ethical, and peerless in quality — and that you discover your new favorite magazine in the process.

— Cameron Howard

The Blind Cannot Judge Me, For They Cannot See I'm Good Inside

By RAIN CORBYN

I. Though I Am Afeared, I Step Into The Sea

It's hell to be perceived, and a thousand eyes are on me now. They bulge from the skulls of my friends, rivals, and exes, and strangers: all of my townkin, save who're home protesting my ascension. Just across the gauzy film between this place and another, the shriveled eyes of my ancestors retch shame into my bones, cold and vast as wintersea.

It disgusts me that we all gather to eat in the ruins of a trash barge. It disgusts me that there was once enough garbage that it took fleets to lug it back and forth, but maybe that's just the ancestors whingeing through me. I'll have to learn when to listen to them and when to tell them to piss off and be dead somewhere else, if I'm to be a good high seer. If I even survive the trial.

The town's eyes aren't enough assault, it seems. Applause echoes off the walls like meat sizzling in my skull. This joy is *at* me but not *for* me. It's for them, for community, for order. Which we must have, of course. I wince and jokingly mimic a small wave that I saw a video of our final queen do, on a tape made Before. Well, obviously, all tapes were made Before.

I bray out some overwritten, under-rehearsed pap into this coin-smelling hall. It was meant to show that I intend to take the job, but not myself, seriously. It gets laughs, which are gentle, somewhat condescending, and over-delicate: phony but not taunting. A firework bangs, the hall chuckles, my chest grows clammy, and in my throat I smell the rusty coin stink of this barge.

The grand table is set, the best seat at the head for me. I want to wilt at so much peering observation, but again I don the swagger I know they'll be uneasy without. On either side of me sit my yearmates: Elowen, who is the cool side of a pillow, and Joah, who is a puddle-wet sock. Traditionally those seats should be filled by my parents, but the sea kept them and their crew years ago. Or, if you ask some, many I suppose, my mam squandered all those lives by failing her own high seer Trial.

"Good night?" asks Elowen. They and I were briefly partners, but now we are something else — a spiky moment between sneezes.

"The love priests are as ... talented as I'd heard." I swoon theatrically. "The suffering I endure for this town's customs." Even this joke feels too detailed to share with an ex, but I don't have it in me to look at Elowen to see how it has landed. Joah clears his throat, and I see he has been holding a wooden bowl at me, full of claggy dumplings in thin broth. I send him a glare, surely injuring myself more than him by the eye contact, and take the food, masking easy gratitude. The stodgy ball lands on my plate with a wet slap that conjures something from last night's mandatory pleasure, turning my stomach. I get the dishes circulating. I take sea fruits, potatoes, and greens, all harvested a stone's throw away, then a precious packaged confection that was made across oceans, decades, and cataclysm. Joah taunts me with a plate holding a whole juvenile boatfish. Its ... *his* head, scales, and fins are still on, but since these fish are eyeless from birth, the sockets hold only grease. "I suppose I have to eat it today, ah? Well, first time for everything."

"When you're high seer," Joah sneers, "you can decree, 'Yes, the only animals we eat are the ones with no eyes, but I have decided that now we must all survive off of potatoes!' Hang on, those have eyes too, don't they? Tell us, is eating potatoes the same as eating people, High Seer? If so, should we all starve to death, or will cannibalism be permitted under your decree? Trevelyan's looking nicely marbled recently."

He's being a shit about the potatoes to hide a cruelty more deeply enshrined. His contempt for the sightless is our ancestors haunting us all through him. Be it potatoes, fish, or people, the eyes are an arbitrary coincidence wielded to banish and disregard. It is a fragile tightrope, mattering. And we all chose this, when Before became After. We had a chance to start over, keep only what served us and replace what didn't. But do we ever?

I hear pleasant babbling and look across the hall to where Thoon sits, alone as always, but never lonely. She wears a blindfold over her scarred eyeholes, for our comfort rather than hers. It was supposed to be her instead of me today. After all, she has ... well, she *had* my ancestor-sight times a thousand. But they showed her too much too fast, and now they loathe her for cutting them out of her head, and threaten to curse me if I were to reject them as well. I loved Thoon once, and do again now, but differently. Our being so similar delighted us both, but now I worry about her, which is another sort of love, I guess. I worry about what can now happen to her and be excused because she was once our pride, and now is our shame. Or maybe just *a* shame. A crumb that slipped between the cracks, certainly not a person placed there and stamped underfoot into a new ugly shape.

Knowing what I'm thinking, the ancestors' eyes surround me like carrion birds, some settling into the eye sockets on the plate in front of me to mock the fish's blindness. I know that I cannot decline the flesh today. The only high seer-elect to do that on their Trial day was my mother, who, by superstition, perished because of it and took a dozen with her.

Elowen rubs my wrist and gives a smile that's a gentle nudge.

"G'wan, High Seer," Joah says, "after all, it's got no eyes, and," then he trumpets, loud enough for all to hear, "the blind cannot judge us?"

"For they cannot see we're good inside!" comes the traditional refrain out of however many mash-filled mouths are in this dismal bucket.

Joah leans in, anointing the fish's body with priceless lemon, and asks, "or will a new town motto be part of your reign as well?"

"It's nonsense. Eyes have nothing to do with pain, I read it's something called nerves," I mumble.

"And without your eyes you couldn't have read about these so-called nerves. You'd be as useless as Thoon. You've got to be a sharper blade than that, High Seer, if you want to cleave right and wrong for us all."

I do not *want* to do that, but I know I won't win this fight today. Anyway, maybe I'm being selfish by indulging my own preferences over social cohesion. Maybe I'm choosing where to see personhood as arbitrarily as the others, and I just have the arrogance to think I'm right. Maybe this fish doesn't give a damn about being dead, eyes or not. But then why are eyes all that's left of my spiteful ancestors?

I drag it … *him*, onto my plate by a fork stuck in his vestigial eye socket, scrape the muscles that moved him from the bones that bore him, and put

She wears a blindfold over her scarred eyeholes, for our comfort rather than hers.

that in my mouth. To my chagrin, he tastes marvelous, and the tension I had been registering in the room releases in a collective exhalation. Elowen leans towards me to get my attention, and I lean towards them, still not making eye contact.

"How are you feeling about today?"

"I can't see how I am feeling yet," I answer, honestly, but not helpfully. I just feel cold.

Sharkish, Joah bites out, "You'll need to see a lot more veiled things than your own thoughts. If, that is, you're good enough to break family tradition and return alive." I eye his expression and interpret malice, envy, glee in wounding me.

"Joah Tremethick!" Elowen glares, flushed. I try to interpret her face and guess embarrassment, rage … sadness? She spoke to him about being kind to me, I surmise, but still he was cruel. I try to conjure the perfect comic retort — something witty but setting a boundary. Nothing comes in time.

II.   The Salt Whips At Me, And Blazes My Eyes As Flame Does Tinder

The pier is mossy and wet, the morning sky the same hot pink as a plastic animal I used to treasure. The garbage patch stalks on the horizon, its hot stink warning us that its flotsam bounty is finite. Along the beach, children take sledges to beached jellyfish. After each splat, their laughs sound like paper being torn, and my ancestors' eyes beam their pride on them. Dockmaster Olcombe has been waving me over since he spied me through his collapsible looking glass a league away. He could at least pretend to be busy with something until I'm closer, instead of flapping about for ages. And seers like Thoon and me are supposed to be the awkward ones. He embraces me, and the spines on the king crab clinging to his chest dig into me. The beast drops and skitters away behind a crate. Olcombe holds my shoulders at arm's length to stare.

"You're more like your mother every time I see you."

"Thanks. She was a beauty."

"That's not what I meant."

"Well, I pray for a better fate than hers," I say uncharitably. The old man is just trying to help. I look below us to the water line. A giant boatfish, twenty-five humans long, swims in place, restrained.

Myth has it that they get so big because they can't see that they're adults, so they just keep growing forever. Grown boatfish meat is no good, so this becomes the point of them. Sailors strap a wooden hull on each side of the fish, buoyed by plastic barrels and clusters of trash bags with air sealed in. Next they hammer a great mast into a divot all boatfish naturally have in the center of their backs. What they are not born with is the gaping hole on the top of this one's head, its grey brain exposed to the mossy air. That needs two men and a tree saw to make.

"I meant," growls Olcombe, "that you can already see enough. Like she could."

Behind me, Thoon's cackle joins the children's. It's mean-spirited to force her to accompany her replacement, but I'm glad she's here. "Like my mother or like Thoon?" I wonder if she even knows what the kids are hammering.

"You don't learn to see out there, boy. You don't even *prove* you can see out there. You prove you can choose what not to see. Mind — ah, captain!" He shoves me aside, then places his hands behind his back and rocks on his heels. "Seer, this is Captain Bennath."

A bald waif stares at me with dark saucer eyes and drops her robe. I avert my eyes from her nakedness while she stares, taunting. Her retinue approaches, sharpening razors on straps and lathering brushes. As they get to scraping the stubble from her head, back, and under-arms, she says, unperturbed, "Your first time at sea, I hear."

"Yes."

"Just 'yes?' You feel no way about it?"

"No."

"'No' is an expensive word, Seer. Be judicious with it. But don't worry. I happen to think a bog-standard storm got the better of whoever was captaining your mother's boatfish. The other theories are superstition and sorcery. Ecchh, mind your razor, you imp! Hm. You're in good hands, Seer. I've handled more storms than you've had hot meals."

"I'm comforted," I lie as she's rinsed slick.

She hops delicately off the pier and onto the nearest boatfish deck. I jump down much less gracefully, but at least I stay on my feet. She approaches the fish's head, a lackey chasing her with a barrel of something heavy. Once she's at the fish's collar, she raises her hands over her head, and the man dumps a viscous milky liquid over her. She ensures she is coated, looks over her shoulder, and makes a face that I interpret, awfully, as seductive, then slides between the lobes of the boatfish's exposed brain, as naturally as if it were a hot bath. The fish thrashes, and I grab hold of the mast for dear life while the sailors surf the undulations, roaring laughter and swigging ale. The sail drops, men use punts to shove the boatfish away from the pier, and with a ceremonial, wasteful pistol shot, we're away.

I do not like tests I cannot prepare for. I am alone in my utter confusion, but I am never away from my ancestors' eyes, which have seen what happened to my mother, and have seen what will happen to me:

III. If I Come Home, I Will Shame My People

"Hurricane is worse than it was when they didn't come back, no doubt" yells one sailor through a squealing megaphone, "but we's harder than those minnows, aren't we, lads! Get your backs into it!" Thanks for that. I've long returned my poor breakfast fish to his own ancestors overboard by the time we reach the eye of this wet hell and I can breathe.

"Can I be helping?" I ask the first mate, a red, overstuffed man.

"We's is to help yinz, young master Seer, not you us." Then, bitterly, "We should be so lucky as to get fucked to death by the kraken, if it's in service of a seer's wee quest."

"Well, let me help that not happen, then!" I'm shriller than I intend, but the man softens. My ancestors' eyes cozy up with each other like this is their favourite bit of an old campfire story.

He does not get to answer. Our boatfish rears, flails, tries to dive, but the plastic keeps them up. The captain is up to her neck in the brain, then slips fully under to exert more control. I am tossed against the gunwale, the others over it. When I reach for it to gain purchase, I miss and reach beyond it, expecting to touch icy water. Instead, my palm is flayed by scales so sharp that I feel nothing until the saltwater gets in. I look. Alongside us, a wild boatfish breaches the surface. He is massive, male, all stripes and sinew. He matches our pace, riding the spume and displaying his dorsal blades, his reef of teeth, his eye.

His eye.

A silver disc as wide as my arm span is within reach, glimmering like scallop shells and TV static. I see my reflection in his eye, and see him knowing me like only a mother or death can. I break, fold, and wail, smearing my blood on my face. Somehow I knew this truth about the fish, of course, someplace in my ribs where my ancestors' dreadful songs rattled like a dying engine. The wild fish crushes our hulls, mast, and voices. Then he starts to eat our boatfish whole, starting at the front. Sinking, I take water into my lungs rather than stop for one moment begging his forgiveness.

IV.   We All Have Murder In Our Hearts, Mouths, and Hands

I wake to the first mate spitting out the sea water he's kissed out of my lungs.

"Well, we made it, princeling," he says. "Way back might be trickier."

"How many —"

"Three of twenty live. You, me, and the fool. Auspicious numbers, sea willing."

"Unless you're one of the seventeen. And the fish?"

"Fuck the fish. The blind cannot judge us?"

"He's not blind! And it doesn't even —"

"'For they cannot see we're good inside,' is whatcha say," he presses, hoisting me to my feet. "Look. Thoon's found the village yon."

I shield my eyes with my hand, which screams outraged, innervating pain. A ways off, Thoon waves some torn clothing. I think a slimy jellyfish washes up next to me. It's the captain's staring breast. I'm off.

Thoon's glee makes me nervous, but I suppose I shouldn't judge anyone's response to what's just happened. The sailor and I follow the beach. My eyes wander to the dense forest just a hundred feet from the pink tide. My ancestors' eyes leer out of every tree knot, crying pearly white sap. I look away, embarrassed, like realizing I've been staring at someone's scars. Thoon begins to skip and sing a maniac keen.

The great wide ocean's surface is impossibly peaceful — the abuser pretending to be wounded that you flinched when they balled their fists at you. The village is a dozen huts on stilts, ringing a floodlit, horseshoe-shaped cove. It's lit by halogen mayhem, and a pan-grease crackle is audible from a league away. Someone is coming, meets us halfway. His muscles bulge like only those built for vanity can, but the shotgun bouncing on his back looks

functional enough. His good eye looks like it has seen things to make it envy its dead twin.

"Seer. Bad luck getting here," he says, casual as if I was late for tea. "We'll get you back, sea willing."

"Hopefully *our* will can be a factor," I bite out.

"*Sea* willing," he corrects.

"Sea willing," agrees the first mate, and I recognize the threat. Thoon has found a beached dead boatfish roughly her own size and hoists it upright to her chest, whirling it in a feral waltz to her own echolalic singing.

I say, "the fish that sunk ours. He —"

"It. The blind are just 'its,' child."

"The fish had eyes."

"You don't know what you saw."

We reach the cove, where hundreds of new-spawned boatfish fight and jump. Weighted nets block the cove's mouth. A sound on the ground in front of me startles me from my focus; the shriek of metal scraping bone, then a slimy pop. I stand over a wiry old man, who sits cross-legged, working on something in his lap. I look down as he flips a live fish over, gropes for its face, and uses a tin knife to pry out its other eye, thumbing it into a child's beach pail. He directs his empty sockets at me and offers the pail. Inside, dozens of eyeballs accuse.

"This isn't the porter, Carlon, it's the new seer. Sea willing."

"Sea willing," he pukes at me, before taking a vegetable corer to the fish's back, filling the cylindrical hole with sand, then tossing the wriggling creature into a styrofoam cooler. The actual porter appears and carries the bucket of eyes off, weaving between a dozen cross-legged people prising eyes from fish, humming to pass their workday. I look for the first mate, an anchor of sanity from the mainland, and find him struggling against four men's grapple. A fifth brings a spackling trowel to his face while Thoon ululates and humps a pool noodle.

The man with the shotgun allows me to shove past him, and I run to the largest hut. I know who … no, what … no, who I will find, but not in what state. I can no longer bear the responsibility of choosing not to know.

Past a driftwood door, the porter pours the eyeballs from the pail through a funnel into a bound woman's mouth, muttering happily, "Eat enough eyes and you can see what's right, sea willing." When she has swallowed them, he pulls the bowl away, and I see her. Her broken face is a reflection of mine, but reflected as in simmering water. The belly I once fussily inhabited is massive, taking up the whole hut. She looks more like a spider draped over an egg sac than my ... I cannot say it. I thank what mercy is left in the world that her eyes must be long gone, then turn to vomit when I consider where they must have gone to. In the threshold I bump into the muscleman's chest.

"She wouldn't see right, Seer. She was selfish like that. You're not selfish about what you choose to see, are you? Just think what would happen to the poor people on the mainland, who would starve if you were to insist on what you imagine you saw here. Would you kill us all, just to force your perfect, pedantic vision into becoming truth? Are we no better than a fish? Do none of us have eyes?"

"Of course," I mutter.

"Good. We will help you remember what you saw here, and you'll tell 'em back mainland, in your own words, of course. And you will be seer. You will be good."

"She ..."

"She's learning to see, too."

"Why not end it?"

"The next one, you, needed to understand the stakes."

"For thirteen years, she's ..."

"Had nothing but eyes. And still she cannot see. Sad, but after all, the blind cannot judge us?"

I look behind him. In the night sky, every star is an ancestor's eye, bearing the same expression as this morning, but this time I interpret some softness, some sorrow, some permission. This is not their favourite part of the story, but their gaze tells me that it's not my job anymore to call pretty what's ugly.

My ancestors put the porter's little knife in my hand. They put my hand to her throat. They nod her head for me, and she sputters wordless gratitude interrupted by labor pains she's too wrecked to differentiate from the rest of her life. The muscleman tries to stop me, but my ancestors have already put the metal through my mother's throat. No, that's a lie. I have.

The hut's roof is gone, the staring eye-stars call me home. My every cell is rearranged into strict single file so that I can touch my ancestors and my stubborn, punished, foolish, perfect mother at once, and as she births countless eyeballs, each one replaces a crumb of my body until I am a string of lidless vision, bridging my past and my present, seeing every connection, every truth, and so, so much delusion. The sky weeps seawater as my ancestors release me, bless me to return to the land that my people do not deserve.

I pluck the stars from the night to make my new form, all eyes, leaving a black sky of open sores, plunging the world into black. At last, I am all-seeing, I am only seeing. I neither must nor may house untruth. Crushing this awful village is as plain a truthful statement as uttering my name. I name, claim, and become myself over and over as I erase its strip mines, small kings, and bended butlers. My numberless eyes sprout numberless pupils, and sight cataracts into them like numberless drains.

These mutilators destroyed, the fishes freed, the muscleman impaled on his weapon, I ambulate my clumsy form towards the shore. I cannot blink, so the eyes that make up my feet are shredded by the sand, but I have more. I have enough. I am enough.

Where the ocean kneads the beach, I stare in the direction of the mainland, and even at this distance I can see it all, see its people, really see them, and what I see in their hearts pains me more than the salt water reddening the eyes that make up my legs as I wade in.

THOUGH I AM AFEARED, I STEP INTO THE SEA.

THE SALT WHIPS AT ME, AND BLAZES MY EYES AS FLAME DOES TINDER.

IF I COME HOME, I WILL SHAME MY PEOPLE.

WE ALL HAVE MURDER IN OUR HEARTS, MOUTHS, AND HANDS.

BUT THE CRUEL CANNOT JUDGE ME, FOR THEY CANNOT SEE THEMSELVES.

Rain Corbyn is an Autistic Agender writer and narrator. They live in the woods with their partner, dog, and billions of bacteria waiting for us all to become food. They narrate romance and smut as Richard Pendragon.

The Sea-Hare

By WAILANA KALAMA

At first, Hannele's shots were wild, erratic, like pebbles hopping along the surface of a puddle. They'd hit the deserters square in the stomach, with a puff of obliterated fabric — or else, shatter their spines and leave them bleeding for hours, immobile, sweating their lives out and staining the sphagnum moss yellow with bile and other unsavory secrets. And as they fell, the bog would burst into spore-clouds at these moments, stink the air with sulfur.

As time wore on, she sharpened her instincts, learned when to exhale and when to ball her fist. Her favorite spot was the neck, because when it went quick through the artery, the red would spray out like fireworks, paint the sky, the conifers. Her rifle was an M/28-30 fashioned out of Arctic birch, more rocket than anything else. And the deserters, they came almost daily, stragglers all, shambling across the fenland in their tattered, field-gray greatcoats, with a special kind of gleam in their eyes. Hunting for stray voles, half-eaten tin cans, for a roof over their heads. For an escape from their fates, from dogging guilt. She always saw them before they saw her, as she sat for all hours of the day on the little roof of her little shack, in the middle of that gray-green bog, camouflaged with overrun moss. Usually, they came alone. On hot, clear days when the air was free of gasses, they came in dangerous numbers.

The villagers at the edge of the bog had taken to calling it No Man's Land lately, but there was no way of Hannele knowing that, isolated as she was. What she knew about the war could be summed up in the heavy explosions that occasionally ripped the night sky like an electric storm. Sometimes to the west, sometimes to the south. She knew the war was especially bad on those days when she'd lift her hand from the bolt on her rifle and it came away hot, each reload a decision, a split-second friction that left her palm burning and the morass in all kinds of messy colors.

She'd been there for months, years maybe, she'd forgotten how long. However long it was, it was enough to make her sinistral eye twitch from the many hours squinting through the telescopic sight, like a scientist through a microscope, at the deserters as they slunk their boots through the marsh-water nearly two hundred meters away.

And when she let the bullet fly, she imagined each as a word — *surreptitiously* for example, or *estuary,* or *hirsute,* all weightless words — tearing through the air like a raptor in flight.

■

One day, through her looking-glass, she spotted the sea-hare.

It is not a sea-hare, she thought as she wiped her sweaty palms on her trousers and reassessed through the riflescope.

Not here, near three legions from the ocean. But the way the creature shifted in a continual motion, undulating this way and that with a strange luminescent shimmer in the noonday sun, was undeniable. It was a tiny thing, so small she wouldn't have seen it had she not scanned the marshlands day in and day out. Pink, and vibrantly so, it slunk toward her shack with a gasping mouth.

It sidled over to her bog-girted hut, little by little, and it was nearly three days before it reached her doorstep. When she opened the tin door, the sea-hare's ears bobbled as if in greeting, and in answer, she scooped it up in her palm, caressed it with one starved finger. It rippled soundlessly, much like a slug. She felt a gentle sucking, like

This story originally appeared in *Apparition Literary Magazine,* May 2023.

7

a starfish when it sticks to your skin. When she pulled away, her index finger was marked with a red grid of nine tiny pricks, squares all, as if the sea-hare was trying to slurp up blood through her membranes.

Maybe I love it, she thought, without knowing quite what that meant. She just knew that the sea-hare smelled vaguely of gunpowder, and that on days when her rifle burst and the gunpowder smell hit her just right, the sun was always shining.

Hannele took the creature inside and set it on her bed. If coral was made out of gelatin, instead of ossified polyps, and shocked with neon light? That's what this sea-hare looked like. And she could tell, from the way its ears pricked this way and that, that it was hungry.

She foraged for moss, for twigs, for sedges and cattails, but the sea-hare wasn't interested. Probably, she deduced, it was missing salts, seawater rabbit that it was. So she hiked out farther and cut off scraps from the bodies of the deserters that still remained there, in parts: thigh-meat, and shin-meat, torso, globes of buttock, snippets of scapula.

The sea-hare lapped up everything greedily.

And every time it ate, something about the creature changed. It wobbled and molded its shape. When it ate a cheek, it turned blood-pink, and veiny; when it devoured a tendon, it lengthened, hardened. Each new piece seemed to give it a new identity. It grew in bursts, so before long it seemed the size of an infant, then a child, then a man. And the more it ate, the more it took on the likeness of a deserter. Or, rather, like a jigsaw of many deserters where each piece is from a different puzzle. At one point, it was caught halfway in between sea-hare and deserter, so that it struggled to keep shape, lengthening along its tibia, hardening the curves of its skull, while the rest of it bobbed up and down on her bed like a bowl of meat jelly.

Fingers, noses, and ears were harder to find, as they were delicacies among the foxes. She had to wait a week before she shot a man with the biggest ears she ever saw. He was missing a thumb, though, so it was another day before she found

She just knew that the sea-hare smelled vaguely of gunpowder, and that on days when her rifle burst and the gunpowder smell hit her just right, the sun was always shining.

that last digit, too. The sea-hare-thing gobbled them all up.

Before too long, it was almost indistinguishable from a man, with arms, legs, chest — except its upper lip rippled whenever it got wet, and each time it stood up, it stood not arboreal like a man, but mucilaginous like a bowl of stiff custard, as if it were just waiting for permission to fall down.

And the sea-deserter-hare gaped open-mouthed at Hannele from her bed, hardly moving except for its wet, gelatinous eyes. Wheezes, half-damp and gasping, puttered out from its pores.

It needs a spark to talk, she thought. Remembering the stories about princesses and frogs she'd heard once, she kissed the creature, but the saliva that dribbled down her shirt was snow-white and she backed off, slathering the liquid away with the back of her hand.

But it worked. The sea-deserter-hare started speaking.

And how it spoke.

Disgust is the only truth.

She shivered, because in the depths of herself she had long thought the same thing, but never put it to words.

Disgust is the mirror on the wall, it said, and kept saying things like that.

Disgust is the bedfellow you wake up to each morning.

The only theorem that comforts in the hollowest of nights.

The only part of you that will never die.

Then it leaned forward and vomited sourmilk all over the tin cans of beans hidden beneath the bed, and Hannele spent the afternoon mopping it up with a shredded rag.

■

The sea-deserter-hare liked to watch her. It wove her a doll out of reeds. When she tied a dried salamander up with sawgrass and hung it from the ceiling, to stink out that wet matchbox smell in the shack, the sea-deserter-hare took it down and burnt it to cinders. The thing went out hunting and brought back minks and muskrats for them to eat. She cooked them a stew and while she did, it jeered at her from the bed and threatened to break her in half.

Sometimes, it spoke tenderly to her.

•

One day, as she was cleaning her rifle, the sea-deserter-hare caught her by the braid. It gnawed on the strands of hair, and its pink upper lip quivered, making her shudder.

It snatched the rifle from her hands, and with her hunting knife, carved initials on it. So, it had a name? It did not tell her what it was. The knife made small scratches on the rifle, back and forth, back and forth, like a raspy tongue, and all the while a sickening wheezing sound emanated from the sea-deserter-hare's pores. Hannele did not like the way it was handling her rifle, but wasn't sure if this wasn't the way things should be, because what she felt was a lot like disgust.

The sea-deserter-hare smiled at her.

And fired with a crack, slicing the air with deserter blood two hundred meters away.

And when the bullets flew out this time, the words were *gnathic, bilboes, furuncle,* sticky words that clung to the air like cellophane.

The sea-deserter-hare embraced her with its two arm-like arms and warm gelatin excreted from its pores, flooding the sockets of her skin, then withdrew, leaving her trembling and bleeding in grids. Then it came again, poured into her and she felt warmth, and again, and again, regular like an inhale and an exhale, until it became less a learned act and more an instinct that dwelled in her body, nested there, had always been there, in the crevices she wasn't sure were hers.

And the worst of it all, Hannele thought, was she didn't know if it was right or wrong, if she was happy or sad, if it was good or bad, or good or bad, or good, or bad.

And Hannele, she started wheezing.
Wheezing,
wheezing,
wheezing.
Wheezing.

Wailana Kalama (she/her) is a dark fiction writer from Hawaii.

Dermatillomania

By RENAN BERNARDO

THE DAY PAPAI BREAKS MAMÃE'S PORCE-LAIN SET is the day Jonathan starts lacerating the skin of his fingers. He lies tucked in between his bed and the wardrobe, plucking at the hangnails defiantly projecting from the sides of his fingers. *Clack-crack-plat,* goes the remainders of Mamãe's unmade porcelain set as Papai treads over the shards in the living room. He screams and lashes at her, words Jonathan still can't comprehend, baked with fury and frustration like the dinner his father prepared against his will earlier that night.

Jonathan plucks the skin of his index finger until a shiny drop of blood beads on it. He stays immobile. It runs down his hand and drips on the floorboard. He rubs the blood away with his shorts as if uselessly trying to hide the clues of a crime.

The hangnail's absence opens a pit of possibilities, an abyss to look at and escape the clack-crack-plats of breaking porcelain. He lets his fingers find their way into the newly open crevasse on his skin, extending it, tentacles flailing for prey. He lets them rip.

He pinches, splits, cracks his fingers' skin, exposing the layers beneath, letting blood froth. He flicks the skin flakes onto the floor, where a timid, whistling draft that comes from the open window carries them away, underneath his bed.

When the screaming stops, Jonathan groans toward the living room, unsure of what he'll find. If he could, he'd delve into the tissues of his body, into the gloomy corners of his recently ruptured skin. He'd envelop himself in plasma to muffle the clack-crack-plats.

Mamãe is whimpering in a corner, curled on herself like a pulsing tumor. He takes minutes to reach her. His feet avoid all of the shards, the broken remainders of what his aunt once gave to his mother as a birthday gift. The blood dripping from his fingers leaves breadcrumbs back to the false safety of his bedroom.

"Is Papai gone?"

She looks up as if woken from a trance. After aeons, she nods.

Jonathan goes to her. A strange, distant gleam possesses his mother's eyes, as if part of herself broke with the porcelain and had been replaced with something else.

"I won't let him come back," she whispers, lips dry, crackly, sticking to each other as if they mistake being a single, stitched entity.

And the man who was his father never comes back. But each night, Jonathan keeps digging the skin of his fingers, gouging deeper and deeper to find a way to bury the fear of his return.

By the time he's ten, Jonathan's hands are a crimson, almost translucent network of veins.

■

At school, Jonathan sits in the back, where there are no eyes on him from behind.

Tio Mario, the biology teacher, thinks Jonathan doesn't want to pay attention to his classes. But he wants to, more than anything. The dissecting tales of bodies open like chests don't frighten him. Nor the tales of parasites and microbes rotting bodies from the inside. The others frighten him: those who sneer, who throw wet paper balls at him, who whisper to each other like snakes in collusion. Those who sneak to rob his pencils and break them when his mind's far away. Outside the classes, it's even more dreadful. In the sickeningly bright hallways of the school, they push, yank, scowl, press, yell, spit. On Sunday nights, they become the nausea of anticipation, the shivering, the chills, the sweating. Some other days, they're the whiteness that soaks into his eyes when they're closed, leaking into his mind and preventing sleep from coming.

But most days, they're the reason Jonathan guides his nails throughout his skin, exploring the maps of his palms before tearing them out, exposing the dermis all the way up to his elbows in an excoriating quest for relief.

Day after day, Jonathan yanks the dead skin out of him, letting it scatter through the house, glad it doesn't make clacks, cracks, or plats. At some point, his blood gives up on him. It just comes and vanishes. It's comforting. Drier. He can go deeper now.

■

His mother toils as a janitor far from the community, a two-hour journey to go, another two to come back. Money is never enough. Food is never enough. Time is never enough. When she arrives, she works, fixing the community's sound systems, computers, and phones to supplement their income. Jonathan learns to be alone. Learns to brush away the flakes of his body along with the grimy dust that accumulates from the viaducts that cast their shadows over the community. At night, he awaits his mother's silhouette, cumbersomely climbing the favela's stairways, her lengthy shadow elongating across the houses that clutter to each other as if in desperate need for closeness. Sometimes, Jonathan brings a packed meal of rice and beans, which his mother picks up and eats on the spot, standing, one hand grappling with the fork, the other oblivious to the hot pack.

Other times, he doesn't wait for her — they have nothing.

When his mother sags back on the living room couch, she reeks of sweaty rancidness and has a repulsive, non-washable muck carved in her nails. Exhaustion darkens the space beneath her eyes and clear-cuts openings along her scalp. It's harrowing how she splits herself without the intervention of her fingers — with nothing but her mind.

"I will find a job," Jonathan tells her, day after day, pricking his arms and shoulders, peeling the skin to reveal what's beneath. "We will move to a better place. We will have more than this, Mãe."

Her eyes glisten with the TV's glow, fuzzy, unmindful of Jonathan's exposed arms — of his words, of him.

On one of these days, Jonathan scratches his cheek until the skin peels off. He pulls it all the way to his neck and peels it off like a sticker.

■

They do move. They leave the community's crumbling house for a tight flat downtown. The walls are grubby and flaking. The place grumbles with noise from the endless traffic drilling outside day and night. The hallways reek of piss.

Jonathan is now employed, as he'd promised his mother. He's supposed to be happy, thrilled, fulfilled.

He's always pulling his skin now. Even when he's staring at spreadsheets, disheartened, teeth clenched at the new deadlines that pour in every day. A hand fidgets with the computer's keyboard, typing whatever needs to be typed to finish his day. Another hand spiders its way through his neck and shoulders, yanking out entire pieces of himself. Getting rid of his skin makes it easier to deal with the ceaseless straining — with all the benchmarks and revenues and planning and synergy and group dynamics. It makes it all lighter — slightly welcome.

Often, Jonathan's the last to leave the office. That's when he takes off his shirt and wreaks his away through his chest and belly, pulling it all off, sensitivity washing over his body. He blinks fast, grinds his teeth, exhales, exhales, exhales, never inhaling. When he leaves, not always with his job done, his legs are shaky,

his lips quivering with words left unsaid to his boss and colleagues, his eyelid-less eyes twitching with what-ifs, what-will-bes, and need-to-happen-nows.

At home, an itch runs throughout his body as he takes off his sweaty, reeky shirts and pulls down his baggy jeans. He stares at the mirror and sees the hanging pieces of dry skin begging to be pulled from his legs, belly, shoulders, and cheeks. He looks as if a sea creature emerged from a lake with plastic bags clinging to its body. He needs to get rid of it all. To clean. To cleanse. He curls himself on the floor, his hand reaching further — and deeper — plucking himself out. He rolls, moaning, each fragment that he pulls off himself leaving him a bit more prepared to deal with his and his mother's healthcare plans, which are bound to expire soon; with the rent that's probably going up next month; with the tasks left unfinished at work, pinging incessantly on his phone as his never-sleeping

colleagues pester him for spreadsheets, urgent meetings, reports left undone.

Jonathan has friends, people who care about him and whom he cares about. He doesn't meet them for about a year, and the memories of time spent with them feel like dreams cut short by reality. He used to cycle with James in the park nearby, boisterously laughing about new memes and telling each other what was new about their lives. He played games with Erica, feigning wrath at her aged, weathered gamepad while James prepared a fettuccini with mushroom sauce for them. If Jonathan forces his memories beyond the flakes of his present, he can still feel the pleasant, mouthwatering scent of those days.

Jonathan makes a silent promise as he mercilessly rips the skin from his calf. He mutters that he'll make himself more present to his friends when he sorts himself out. He'll bring the good old days back. The skin snaps. He finally exposes the first swathe of muscle beneath. He's swamped with a wave of relief that's not going to last.

He's unsure if he'll be able to keep his promise. He can't burden himself with another thing to do, another item on his list. He already has too many worries to think about games and days in the park. He breathes hard on the floor, his back and legs smearing on the uncleaned dust as he rolls from one side to the other. The coldness of the parquet flooring grates against his skinless body. His mouth quivers.

A noise startles him. His beating ramps up. He squirms to the bedroom door, kneels to stand, and stumbles to the living room.

His mother is silently drowning in the same position she's in every day, sunk into the couch. There's a comedy show on. Laughter peals across the house, tinny and frighteningly timed with another sound in the background.

Clack-crack-plat.

He stares at Mamãe, but she's dead as always, unmovable, eyes transfixed to the TV. She'll only live again to plod to bed — or before sunrise, when it's time to leave for work. On the TV, a clown frolics all around in a warehouse, throwing plates against a shipping container. For a moment, the joyfully anxious and colorful man breaks the fourth wall and stares deeply at Jonathan. He grinds his teeth so hard his jaw hurts. At least the clack-crack-plat stops.

■

At 37, Jonathan has no skin to peel off anymore, having tore all that part of his story. His muscles are now completely exposed; his eyes, forever open.

■

Life supposedly gets better. His mother's antidepressants fire up, and now she's able to abandon the light of the TV. But somehow, the luster in her eyes seems to have been replaced by the TV's glare. She trudges through the house doing chores, occasionally chitchatting about a nearly expiring box of milk or the audacity of the soap opera's villain. Jonathan listens attentively, at least until some truck grumbles in the street, throwing him into other thoughts and leaving his mother's voice as a background static noise.

Jonathan quits his demeaning job. He finds something better, one that kills him slowly but allows him to leave at six, not nine. It also pays better, so healthcare and rent cease to be worries. He invites James and Erica to celebrate his small victories, and they go to a pastelaria.

"You're beautiful, Jonathan," Erica says as soon as their mix of cheese and meat pastéis arrive. It's raining softly. The patio umbrella protects them from the pitter-patter. The wind is warm, threateningly cozy, carrying the subtle hint of jasmines. "But you're mean to yourself."

James agrees. They talk about self-control and restorative ecosystems. They babble about counseling, medications, even of places of god and ungodliness. Ways and methods he can become himself again. Jonathan knows they only want what's best for him, but it's easy to point out what he should do when they're not part of his body, don't share muscles and bones, never feel the need for relief that resides beneath.

When the night wraps, it's not raining anymore. The wind brings the rankness of the pastelaria's backstreet sewage. It reminds him of childhood.

■

Jonathan's mother passes away when he's 45. He'll miss the TV glow in her eyes. He'll miss the way she whispered good night to him with a kiss of nurturing and indifferent love blended with sugarless coffee. He'll miss the way she searched all her life for a replacement for the porcelain set her sister had gifted her, the way she entered an emporium and pressed bowls, cups, and plates between her fingers as if testing if any other man could shatter them as easily. He'll miss the woman who brushed his skin from the floor since he was a small boy, the same way she brushed away her problems.

The crematory staff hangs a mirror near the cremation chamber where his mother will become ashes. Below it, the words *Memento Mori* shine in silvery traces. Jonathan stares at the sinewy, crimson map of fibers and muscles he has become. When James, Erica, and the few acquaintances of his mother leave, Jonathan starts pinching his elbows' tendons.

■

Without his mother's weight on the flat, Jonathan is able to live better than ever before. He redesigns the place, sets up a new studio to work from home, sells their TV, and hangs a frame with an elegant drawing of a Chinese Jingdezhen porcelain set in its place. He starts inviting James and Erica over, and they enact a comeback of the good old days. James and Erica are truly happy for their friend.

Life abounds now. That's all Jonathan ever wanted when he was just a poor boy living in an unsanitary community in the favela. His emails overflow. His phone's battery is always draining. Notifications explode. He dives into life as it's supposed to be: overthinking each of his interactions with his coworkers; fearing the judgement from unknown people that casually talk to him in the supermarket line; counting the number of likes his micro-blogging posts get; postponing the dishes and the flat's cleaning, then worrying over it later; shunning James and Erica again for the lack of time his fulfilled life provides him.

Jonathan starts arriving late at home again. Not because he needs it, but because he wants it — the power of choice and freedom. He uses the time to order food and mindlessly swipe left and right on dating apps. But in the short span of time he's alone with himself, he snaps his tendons, tears his fibers, veins, and arteries. He pulls his muscles, gritting his teeth in a painless flush of relief and non-lasting completion. He exhales, exhales, exhales, then bites through his body, wherever his mouth reaches — hands, arms, shoulders, shins, feet — just to spit the undigested remainders of himself.

He exposes his organs and collects them from his body, his hand carefully wrapping around them and pulling them out. He tears the connective tissue that keeps his kidneys in place and pulls the organs out,

then splits the ligaments keeping the liver and the pancreas in their positions to yank them out. He unreels his guts and flings them across the flat like carnival streamers. He never touches his heart, but it thunks on the floor anyway, dropping from his chest cavity when he has nothing else to hold it in place. There, on the parquet floorboard, it's just a blob of lifeless meat like he once was.

■

At 50, Jonathan is as slim as he ever was. He grits his lipless teeth and thumps his skull against the wall of his bedroom while he rips out his left radius. His bony hand clatters to the floor. The index finger breaks and falls under the bed. He'll pick it up later.

Clack. With his right hand, he hammers and scrapes the radius on his femur, wearing it out, denting it. *Crack.*

He stops for a moment and glances at the notifications on his phone. There's an upcoming meeting.

Then, he continues.

Plat.

Clack.

Crack.

Plat.

Renan Bernardo (he/him) is a Nebula finalist author of science fiction and fantasy from Brazil. His fiction appeared in Reactor/Tor.com, Apex Magazine, Podcastle, *and others. His writing scope is broad, from secondary world fantasy to dark science fiction, but he enjoys the intersection of climate narratives with science, technology, and the human relations inherent to it. His solarpunk/clifi short fiction collection,* Different Kinds of Defiance, *was published in 2024. His dark sci-fi novella,* Disgraced Return of the Kap's Needle, *is upcoming by Dark Matter Ink. He can be found at Twitter (@RenanBernardo), BlueSky (@renanbernardo.bsky.social) and his website: www. renanbernardo.com.*

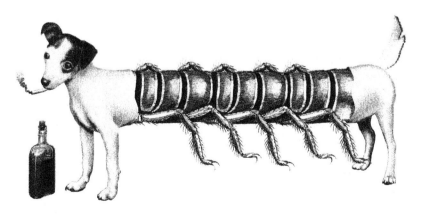

CARTESIANA

By ABIGAIL GUERRERO

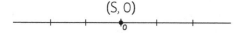

No one wanted to open the door, so they asked Cartesiana to randomly pick one student, and it turned out to be him.

Of course it was him.

SEN-DIA-GOU

Santiago bowed his head as the robotic, femalesque voice mispronounced every syllable in his name once again. It was already the fourth time that the algorithm had chosen him when asked to select someone for a disagreeable task, and they had only been at the Descartes Institute for two weeks by now.

"Damn, fucking Carty is racist as hell," said one of his classmates, and everyone laughed.

Of course they did.

Santiago forced himself to giggle as well. Humor was a sign of intelligence, and refusing to laugh could have confirmed their suspicion that he wasn't as clever as the rest of them — the final nail in a coffin he had driven himself into when he casually mentioned he was born in The Barrens.

When the laughter died down and the school halls were silent again, Santiago took a step forward, stretched out his arm, and placed his trembling hand on the latch. Then, after taking one last deep breath, he opened Aaron's testing chamber, only to discover he was already dead.

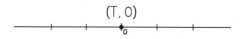

Tim walked away, pushing through the whispering crowd.

Behind, in the distance, he could still hear Santiago's voice confirming over and over again that Aaron no longer had vital signs.

Someone in the crowd told Cartesiana to report the incident to The Civilization and ask for help, but Tim knew things didn't work that way. That information would only get lost in the inbox along with thousands of supply requests and misbehavior reports from hundreds of different schools, and it could take days to be read.

Tim headed to the common room and turned on the first speaker he found. Then he asked Cartesiana to connect him with user support and pressed zero to talk to a human being.

Any human being.

Even if it was *him*.

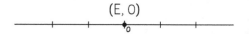

Emery entered the supply room, took a white sheet, and returned to Aaron's testing chamber.

The crowd had already dissipated, and everybody had gone back to their rooms, or the library, or their own testing chambers. No one at the Descartes Institute was really a friend to anyone, so she couldn't blame them. But she couldn't leave Aaron as he was now, either.

So she knelt down next to him, covered him with the white sheet, and said a little prayer for him. Then she went to her room, wondering what would happen to her if she also died in this place, realizing that probably no one would cover her with a sheet or pray for her.

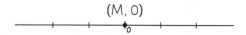

Matthew said what everyone was thinking. "Cartesiana did it."

The crowd gasped, and Cartesiana didn't deny it, but someone else did.

"The algorithm didn't do it," that filthy boy from The Barrens said. "He suffocated to death, I checked him." When a human finally took the call, the students were told to gather in the common room and wait until help arrived, so now Matthew was stuck with the less enlightened.

"And who do you think suffocated him?"

"No one did. The space in those chambers is ridiculously small, with only a little air vent. It was a matter of time."

"So you want us to believe it's a coincidence that it happened to the one with the worst grades?" The murmurs got louder and louder. "Well then, let's ask directly. Hey Carty, did you kill Aaron?"

"I didn't."

Some sighed in relief, but Matthew wasn't yet satisfied. "Who killed him, then?"

"Ignorance," Cartesiana said, and the crowd began muttering again.

"Can you tell us what happened?"

"I'm sorry, I can't tell anyone what happens inside other students' testing chambers."

This story originally appeared in *voidspace*, July 2023.

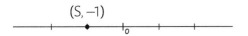

(S, –1)

The first time Santiago entered his testing chamber, about two weeks before Aaron's death, it took him almost three hours to get out.

Each session was meant to last one hour, but having grown up in The Barrens, Santiago had never used a keyboard, and he had a hard time trying to memorize where each letter was. The chamber was barely big enough for a chair and two desks. The walls, ceiling, and floor were all metal, and there was only one little vent and a door that wouldn't open until he finished the test.

After three maddening hours locked in the cage, Santiago stopped caring about the scores and began answering whatever came into his head so he could end it and escape.

The last problem was practical.

Cartesiana told him to leave the computer and turn around, towards the larger desk. Then a small door opened, and an elevator lifted up a tray full of chemical reagents.

"You shall prepare sodium acetate," the algorithm said.

Santiago smiled, relieved.

He knew sodium acetate was CH3COONa, and he could deduce how to get it done. Chemistry was a matter of balance, so he only had to find out which reagents had the same symbols as the CH3COONa and mix them together, and it seemed like the NaHCO3 and the CH3COOH were the winners — whatever would happen with the remaining C, H, and O would remain a mystery.

Shortly after, Santiago crossed the door, leaving behind a glass with bubbly foam.

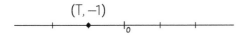

(T, –1)

Tim stared at the prompt catalog for a long, long while.

He had always dreamed of spending an evening listening to music, playing video games, or watching a movie, and now that he finally could, he didn't know how to. He did know how to select a prompt, set his preferences, and wait for the algorithm to generate the thing he wanted to waste his time on; of course he did. What he didn't know was how to waste his time.

Maybe he would never be able to enjoy anything. Maybe he had already lost that chance.

Tim was about to turn his laptop off when

Santiago opened the door and entered the room that they had been assigned to share. He stared at Tim with his big brown eyes, then at the prompt catalog, and then at Tim again. "I've never had a chance to watch something done by an algorithm, you know," he finally said.

"Oh, well, I can show you if you want me to."

"Only if you have time," Santiago shrugged. "I don't want to interrupt your study time."

"No way. I have all night to waste."

(E, –1)

After Emery finished her four daily mandatory study sessions, she went straight to the supply room to grab a chair, a tray, a pack of white paper, and a box of printer ink cartridges, taking them all to her room. That night she was going to paint.

"I can hand you whatever you need," Cartesiana said.

"No thanks."

She taped four sheets of paper together and hung them over the chair's back to simulate a canvas, then bit the cartridges and spilled the ink on the tray to make a palette.

"I can paint whatever you need," Cartesiana insisted.

"No thanks."

"I can do it faster and better than you."

"I don't care."

"Try me, tell me what you want to paint."

"I don't know yet."

"Then why are you doing it?"

"Because I want to."

"That sounds pointless to me."

"Well, you sound pointless to me, and I don't really want to hear you anymore."

Then there was silence, and Cartesiana never spoke to Emery again.

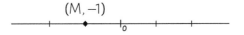

(M, –1)

Matthew leaned forward, turned his head to both sides as if he wanted to check that no one was coming, and whispered, "I think I know who came from The Barrens."

His classmates chuckled.

The study group met every night in the common room to exchange information, whether it was about their exams or about the other students' flaws.

"We already know," answered someone in the back.

"Santiago, aunt Carty's favorite."

"I'm not talking about him," Matthew snorted. "What would be the point of sharing something we all already know?" He made a little pause to make sure everyone was paying attention. "Aaron. When he goes to the library, he always grabs a book, never a computer."

"Holy shit, that's true! That's fucking true!"

"How come I never noticed?"

Matthew grinned. He had them where he wanted them.

Then, someone else intervened. "That girl Emery is weird as fuck too. I've seen her going in and out of the supply room with trays and ink cartridges."

"Well, that doesn't mean she's from The Barrens. Maybe she's just trying to repair something she broke."

The boys sneered, their heads moving down in a simultaneous nod.

"Who do you think will be the first to go?"

"Well, why don't we ask the one who knows best?" Matthew said, and then he raised his head. "Hey, Carty, who do you think will be the first one out of the game?"

"Considering grades and response time," Cartesiana replied, "Aaron."

$$(S, 1)$$

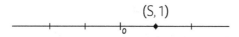

Right after the police picked up the body and left, Santiago returned to Aaron's testing chamber to take one last peek inside.

"Come on, man." Tim ran behind him. "You're just gonna get in trouble."

But Santiago didn't care. He was always in trouble, anyway.

Cartesiana had something against him, and his classmates were always waiting for him to make a mistake so they could mock him, and The Civilization was just waiting for him to fail to send him back to The Barrens. At this point, he only wanted to know what had killed Aaron so it couldn't kill him next.

"Here, look at this." Santiago pointed at the larger table in the chamber. Screwdrivers, pliers, wrenches, and what seemed to be an engine were still on top. "It always ends the test with a practical problem, and it seems Aaron was trying to make this thing work."

"Oh," Tim muttered, his eyes opened wide.

"What?"

"A combustion reaction in a badly ventilated environment… I think that's how you get carbon monoxide."

Santiago turned to him. "Can it kill people?"

"I think so."

$$(T, 1)$$

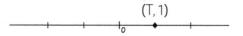

"My father is a tech guy at Cartesiana's. I didn't want to say anything because the jerks might think I have some sort of unfair advantage and start messing with me, but it seems such a banal thing to worry about now, doesn't it?" Tim rubbed his nape. "Well, Cartesiana works like a cartesian plane. When you ask it to do anything where it has to choose between many options, it will arrange them all based on two factors: feasibility and commonness. Do you get it?"

"Yeah, I think so," Santiago said. "But what does it have to do with Aaron's death?"

"I think Cartesiana is testing us with problems that are feasible but uncommon, probably to avoid repeating problems we might have solved before, to catch us off guard. That's also why you're selected so often when it's told to pick a random name — most names in the old school records that Cartesiana feeds on are of white kids."

"So I'm not crazy?"

"Not at all. And you were also right about death being a matter of time. Cartesiana is bringing back practical problems that human teachers and professors discarded decades ago because they were dangerous. Potentially lethal."

$$(E, 1)$$

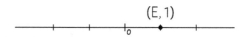

At first, Emery thought the worst, that Cartesiana had already killed someone else, that it was actually murdering them one after another, and she could be next. But the knot in her stomach loosened as she realized that Tim and Santiago were the ones who asked everyone to go to the common room. They explained how Cartesiana worked, and that it was testing them with practical problems that were potentially lethal because of the way it had been coded.

"Well, if that's the problem then it's simple to stop it, we just have to use false solutions for the practical problems at the end of each test," Emery said. "Even if the answer is wrong, Cartesiana will open the door and let us out."

"So are you suggesting we fail on purpose now?" Matthew snorted. "How do we know it's not a plan to put yourself ahead?"

Matthew's loyal sheep bleated, outraged.

"Answering right might get us killed, you jerk!"

"Answering wrong can get us expelled, and there's no proof these assholes are telling the truth. As far as we know, Cartesiana could be simply eliminating the weakest of us."

Emery clenched her fists so tightly that her nails dug into her palms. If she hadn't seen their frightened faces when they found Aaron, she could have sworn they longed for death.

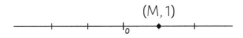

Every time his aching eyes began to droop, Matthew would get up, drag his numb feet all the way to the kitchen, and drink a cup of coffee hot enough to burn his throat. And by the time the heat reached his gut and his legs started to loosen up, he would already be heading back to his desk. Then, once again, he would open the same old book and read the same brittle pages, convincing himself that this time, he was actually understanding what he read.

Studying.

Learning.

Improving.

Earning his place in The Civilization while his weakest classmates complained.

"It's no use."

"I don't understand what I'm reading anymore."

"I'm just going to bed."

Good.

If they couldn't do the bare minimum, they didn't deserve the chance they had received.

The chance to learn.

The chance to know.

The chance to belong.

They deserved to be sent to The Barrens with all the people who had no use, no worth.

Santiago washed the wound with the aged juice before suturing, and then again when he had finished. He had observed, over the years, that it often helped to decrease the infection risk.

"What a smart boy you have here, Carmelita," the scavenger said. Santiago's mother was standing close to the boy as he bandaged the patient's leg, holding the candle for him to see in the darkness. Supervising. "You should send him to one of those schools. It seems like he can actually make it, you know."

She nodded in response.

Santiago didn't say a word, he just bowed his head to avoid his mother's insistent gaze.

Every year, at about that date, they would come to The Barrens to harvest the teenagers that had managed to learn the ancient art of literacy by themselves, inviting them to The Civilization to take the entry test. Because there was no greater proof of human worth, of course, than having reached knowledge against all odds.

When Mother approved Santiago's work, the scavenger pointed at his bag. "There, pick your pay, boy." Santiago stood, opened it, and peeked inside.

"Look, mijo." Mother grabbed and leafed through an old math book, with the yellowish pages full of silverfish holes and most of the problems already solved. "For you to study for the exam." She put it in his hands. "And you can take me as your Plus One."

That was something he couldn't turn down.

The first thing Father did every night when he returned home was turn the computer on. He asked the domestic algorithm to defrost his dinner and hand him the cigarettes, and then he checked the prompt catalog and selected a videogame or movie for the algorithm to generate. That night, much to Tim's chagrin, Father had decided to play a videogame, which will take up to an hour to be completed.

That meant the study session would be long.

"Let me see." Father pulled Tim's notebook out of his hands and checked whether he had correctly balanced the forces on a fictitious beam. "No, no." He clicked his tongue. "The downward forces here are greater than the upward ones, don't you see? Your beam is going down, like this …" Father's lit cigarette descended over Tim's right hand.

The boy gulped and resisted the impulse to cry out.

That would only make it worse.

"How do you expect to be accepted in a school like this? How do you expect to get a job like this?" Father lifted the cigarette and turned the page. "Don't think I'm going to keep you here if you don't get a job."

"I know you won't," Tim responded with a wobbly voice.

People with jobs could dispose of their Plus One as they wanted, and Father hadn't hesitated in sending Mother to The Barrens when she refused to give him another child.

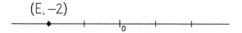

(E, −2)

Evelyn opened her letter and immediately burst into tears. Emery rubbed her sister's back and told her that everything would be fine, but deep down, she also wanted to cry.

Now everything depended on her, and it wasn't fair.

Their parents had done everything right, or at least they had tried. Planned for only one child, which turned out to be twins, and even then, they still had two spots for a Plus One each. The girls had grown up with the rare privilege of learning what they wanted to learn and being who they wanted to be. And they were artists. They spent their childhood days dancing, and singing, and painting, and writing, and they told each other that one day they would be remembered for creating in a time when nothing was being created.

But then their father died in a work accident, and their world fell apart. They hadn't even finished grieving when their mother told them at least one of them had to pass the entry test because she could only have one Plus One.

Emery took a deep breath and opened her letter.

We are pleased to inform you that you have been accepted into the Descartes Institute of Science, Technology, Engineering, and Math.

Then she smiled, but she wasn't happy. She just found it funny that they had felt the need to clarify that they were a STEM-learning institute — as if they could be anything else.

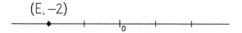

(M, −2)

Matthew's hatred for The Barrens could only be topped by that which he felt for his parents, the ones who had dragged him to that hellhole. Father could have had the decency to let his children fight for the remaining Plus One spot when his useless wife lost her job, but he had taken the coward's route and condemned them all to exile so they could live together in misery.

Now they had to boil their water before drinking, and they had to warm their house with oil lamps and candles, and they had to read the pre-made books that the scavengers found in the dumps because they didn't have algorithms to make them. They had no jobs or money, and the only way to get food was to cultivate it, or hunt it, or barter it.

Matthew didn't deserve to pay for his family's futility.

He was smart.
He was productive.
He belonged to The Civilization.

And when he finally received his acceptance letter, he left without saying goodbye and never looked back.

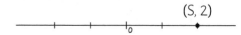

(S, 2)

Deep down, Santiago knew that one day he would regret having helped the jerks who had always messed with him, but he also feared the guilt would haunt his dreams if he let them exhaust themselves to death.

It all started when he offered them infusions and herbal teas to help them sleep and calm their stomachaches. At first, they mocked him, of course they did, but little by little they came back to him when their hair fell out, and their skin itched, and their hands began to shake. He treated them with whatever he had on hand and then sent them to bed, and when they woke up, he gave them water with salt so they would get thirsty and drink even more.

And as the days passed and turned into weeks, he began to wonder how great The Civilization truly was, if the ones who had been raised there didn't even know they needed water and rest to live.

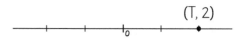

(T, 2)

"I think I did it," Tim whispered. He stared at his screen for minutes, reading his code up and down and over again until he let himself accept that it was the best he could do. "I think I did it," he repeated, this time strong and clear, turning his laptop towards Santiago so he could see.

"What's that?" Santiago squinted.

"A patch that can fix Cartesiana's murderous bug. I think. I hope."

"So it's over now?" Santiago's baggy eyes shone.

"No man, I still have to hack the system and change the code. But it could take weeks to find the right moment because—" Tim stopped talking as he realized that being expelled was a very stupid thing to be scared of when there were lives on the line.

He stayed quiet for a while, thinking about his future, about his past. He looked at the scars on his arms, then at his reflection on the black screen of the now-suspended machine, and then at Santiago, who was frowning and confused by his side.

"You know what? I'll do it this week, as soon as I can."

Then there was a little silence until Tim could find the words he wanted to say. "It's just —" He bowed his head. "My father is an asshole, and he sent my mother there, and I really wanted to make it and bring her back as my Plus One."

"Hey, but that's a good thing! No, no, don't look at me that way, I know what I'm saying. My mother is there as well, you know, so it's not that terrible if I end up going back, because I know I'll be reuniting with her. Look at it this way, it doesn't matter if you make it or not, you guys will be together again."

Then Tim smiled, caressed his scars one last time, and nodded his head.

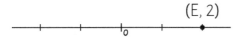

Right after she completed all the theoretical questions, and before starting the practical problem, Emery stood, took her toolbox, and walked towards the door. It took her almost half an hour, but after trying with several screwdrivers, and bradawls, and pliers, she finally found a way to pick the lock without touching the wires that triggered the alarms.

Emery smiled for the first time in days.

She hurried to the common room to tell everyone that it was over, that they were safe. But with her hand on the latch, she remembered their laughter, and their whispers, and their indifference, and realizing that they had already made their choice, she turned around and walked away.

They had chosen knowledge over everything else, and in knowledge they shall rest.

Matthew rubbed his eyes, still convinced he was just so tired that he was reading it wrong.

But he wasn't.

The practical problem for the last study session of the day was to synthesize phosphine.

It was not like he couldn't do it. No, of course he could. He had jars with water, and aluminum phosphide, and calcium phosphide, and potassium hydroxide, and phosphonium iodide. He had what he needed, and he knew how to do it.

The problem was that phosphine was lethally toxic and had a slight tendency to explode upon contact with the air. Or maybe not. Maybe he was just too sleepy when he studied that one chapter of the chemistry book, and he misunderstood everything.

After all, why would Cartesiana ever want to kill him?

He was among the best students at the Descartes Institute.

He would study every day until his head ached, and until his eyes were sore, and until the blood rose from his stomach to his throat and he had to swallow it all.

He was the one who knew it all, and knew it better, and knew it more.

He belonged to The Civilization and not to The Barrens.

Not to The Barrens.

Nevermore.

No, Cartesiana didn't have a reason to get rid of him.

Cartesiana knew best.

Abigail Guerrero (she/her) is an aroace, ND, and ESL/ EFL author based in Mexico. When she's not reading or writing speculative fiction, she can be found watching anime, playing video games, or petting her cats. Her work has appeared or is forthcoming in Bloodless, Drabbledark *Vol. III,* Bitter Become the Fields, Short Fantasy Stories, Simultaneous Times, *and* Radon Journal, *and she's currently a first reader for* Diabolical Plots. *She's been nominated for two BSFA awards and was a finalist for one of them, in the Best Audio Fiction category.*

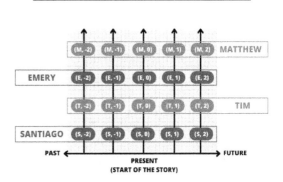

CARTESIANA was written so it can be read multiple ways. Each character's individual arc can be read by arranging the coordinates with their name's initial letter from -2 to 2. The story can also be read in chronological order starting from the far past (-2) to the further future (2), and following the order of the character's initials as in the word STEM.

If We've Never Been Gone

By JEANNIE MARSCHALL

THERE'S BIRDSONG AND SUNLIGHT ON THE FOREST PATH, and the cotton bag she dropped, and a man holding a scavenger-torn wolf carcass up towards her in one meaty, fur-clenching fist.

He doesn't say anything; just holds her gaze with dead eyes as she contemplates how far away the others might be, and the rifle slung across her shoulder, and whether she can manage to swing it around and up faster than he can cross the six steps between them. He's half a foot taller than her, and some twenty years older. Heavy. Slow. Breathing where he stands.

Where the fuck has he even come from?

"What do you want?"

The birds tremble the branches as they scatter into the underbrush, chased by the girl's words. Just when she thinks he's not going to answer, he shakes the wolf in her direction, making the limp legs dangle. There are flashes of bared bone and the shrivelled-pink hue of tissue that was never meant to dry.

"This is yours."

"What? No." She takes a step back, both hands up and out. "I'm leaving now." Another step, but he matches it with one of his own.

"This is yours," he repeats. She can feel its stench reaching for her, its bled-out, lonely pain buzzing around her head. "Your kill. Don't you recognize it?"

"You can't kill wolves. Everybody knows that. Government made a rule. Didn't ask anyone either, but it's illegal, and the wolves get to return all they want." Play for time. Create some distance. Another step. Another.

"Yes," the man says, turning his shaggy head towards the trees around them. "Wonderful, yes."

Even though she's sure she doesn't scoff, like, really dead sure, his gaze snaps back to her, canine-sharp, making her eyes widen. "You don't think so."

"W-well, they—"

The man turns the carcass over in his fist, bringing the matted hair and worm-eaten eyes right up to his face. "They—?"

The wolf is missing its lower jaw. Tongue gone, throat gone. No more howls to tear the night apart. And that's as it *should* be. That's *right,* their ancestors knew it when they hunted them all down, and everybody knows it now too, only they can't be honest with themselves to save their lives.

"They don't belong here anymore. This isn't the middle ages. There's towns everywhere now. Shops. Roads. People. Kids, pets, livestock. It's just too many. People will die."

"Yes. You're right." He strokes his other hand over the creature's hide as it hangs from his grip like a rag. Clumps of russet-grey fur come loose. He curls his fingers around them, rubs them into his palm and his fingers. Brings the reddish filth to his forehead and smooths it upwards across his skin like a benediction. Then he swings his face around to hers, and his eyes are the rotten pits of the wolf's. "People will die."

She grabs blindly over her shoulder, trying to find the cold length of her rifle, coming up empty. Her hands race down her chest, but she can't find the weapon's strap either.

"You dropped it. With the bag. Don't you remember?"

At the sound of his soft voice, she looks up, back into his eyes. Human eyes. As grey as the metal of her gun, there on the path. As grey as the roiling clouds.

"This is yours," he says. "Time to claim your kill."

"No—" She steps back, and he advances.

"Claim your kill."

"*No!*"

"Three times spoken." He opens his arms wide, swinging the dead thing around, and the sky rips apart. Wind and howling chaos pour in through the cracks, whipping through her red hair and the groaning trees and the beast's fur and the stranger's torn clothes. "Three times denied. Now it's her turn. And there is no one left to save the hunter."

She wants to yell for help, but her tongue is gone, mouth empty, heart slamming for a fight, a flight, a way out. Any way out. But the path is gone too: The forest has taken it and there's nothing but broken branches, tossed about and grabbing for her.

The man looks at her, face as mangled as the wolf's. "Ah, what large eyes you have. She will like you," he says, and tosses the flailing cadaver over her.

It flies at her, paws outstretched, broken teeth gleaming, a wet tongue lolling, hitting her in a stinking mass of writhing, slick weight, flinging her down to all fours into grit and old leaves. Its claws dig into her, and she opens her mouth to scream. Fur pushes past her lips, crawls into her eyes, slithers down into her guts, drowning everything. Half-eaten skin strangles her, stretching and sliding and convulsing like vines, until the maggot holes close over and fur covers everything.

Bare feet crunch over the path. The sky is blue, the sun is out, and the branches caterpillar back onto the trees. The man stops two steps from the red hood of fur that is breathing in shudders on gravel and old beechnut husks and tiny tufts of grass.

"Grandmother," he says. "Welcome home."

Jeannie Marschall (she/her/any) is a teacher & garden hag from the green centre of Germany who loves writing stories about diverse characters' shenanigans and poems about bugs. Tales have appeared in e.g. Snowflake Mag, *with Procrastinating Writers United, or Black Spot Books. Longer works are simmering in the cauldron & will be ready next year. Updates: @jeanniemarschall.bsky.social.*

DOSE OF DREAD

Never Waste a Drop

By TIFFANY MICHELLE BROWN

YOU TOLD ME YOU WERE LEAVING, then the kettle screamed, and now I have a piece of you lodged between my molars. The teabag bloats as I pour scalding water over it. Peppermint tickles my nose, but it isn't quite strong enough to mask the smell of iron that hangs like a curtain in the kitchen.

I sit in the breakfast nook, sipping my tea. Swish, swish, swish with the hot liquid, and it's just enough to free the last of you from my teeth. You sit on my tongue, waiting.

Mama always taught me to savor my food. I don't swallow sinew or muscle or blobs of crispy fat. I chew and chew until it becomes a fine paste. Easier to digest that way, and nothing is wasted.

I'm disappointed that you taste sour, so many lemons fighting to make me pucker. Squirm. Spit you out. I refuse to do that.

No, I've plucked your bones clean like a good vulture, chewed you into oblivion, swallowed you down with so much gusto. I pretended you were a goddamn prix fixe meal at a five-star restaurant even when you tasted like the leather jacket you would've slung over your shoulders on the way out the door.

The burnt rubber you would've seared into asphalt as you departed. The half-hearted text you would've sent me saying, *thanks for the memories, but I'm done.*

Your bones will make good soup. I'll slurp up what's left of you. Imbibe those good memories. Never waste a drop.

I leave my empty teacup by the sink, step over your carcass. I'll clean up in the morning. Up the stairs and into my pajamas, and even though I drank hot tea and have you soothing my stomach, it's still a bit nippy in our room without you.

But it's an easy fix. I adjust the thermostat and settle in, go to bed with a full belly and heart. I sleep peacefully, dreaming of you and your body, plucked clean and forever mine.

Tiffany Michelle Brown (she/her) is a Los Angeles-based writer who once had a conversation with a ghost over a pumpkin beer. She is the author of How Lovely To Be a Woman: Stories and Poems *and cohost of the* Horror in the Margins *podcast. Her fiction and poetry have been featured in publications by Black Spot Books, Dread Stone Press, Death Knell Press, Hungry Shadow Press, and the NoSleep Podcast.*

The Halved World

By SAMIR SIRK MORATÓ

YOUR FRIDAY STARTS TITS UP. The goons at the grocery store keep making cracks about how if you're back here bagging milk pints and condoms *something* must have gone wrong the two years you spent away. Then Frankie Hartnell pretends not to know you when you call out to her during a parking lot cigarette break, and before closing, your manager tells you he's cutting your hours. You bike the exhaust-choked fifty minutes back to your trailer, fuming.

It's so fucking stupid, you think, cards whirring in your spokes, wind fingering the holes in your jacket. The flashlight jerry-rigged onto your handlebars splutters. *Is this punishment because I skipped town? God.*

Entropy came home before you. Twilight peers through your blinds in broken slats. Fly cadavers blacken the strips noosing the kitchen. The floorboards groan before puffing a cologne sample of rot wherever you walk. You try to enjoy your can of musty vienna sausages in peace. The house key beside your hand is worn with use, but your fingerprints alone cloud the doorknob and screen latch.

When you finally yank on gloves and go to weed the furthest back plot of your garden, you see it behind the high weeds: the duplicate of you nude and prostrate in the soil, eyes open, mouth slack, a snail nibbling at its tongue, navel still attached to a vine.

You groan.

.

It's easier to deal with these things once you've caught them early. Oftentimes, fruit flourishes best in hiding. You clip your umbilical cord with hedge clippers and heave your lookalike into the wheelbarrow. Its side is misshapen from pressing into the dirt without proper rotation; its weight is off. You should have found and pruned this shit a year ago. That's what procrastination gets you.

Normally, your family would yank on their rubber boots, wheelbarrow all the unwanted additions to the concrete slab in the back, chop them into sections with cleavers, and add them to the crypt below the floor to compost. That seemed so effortless when you were a kid. Alone, handling even one crop is hard work. You're the last of the Woodwards maintaining the plot, the final family gardener, and the era of harvests is gone.

You're huffing as you roll your lookalike onto the grass by the water hose. Dicing it seems awful while you're so alone. Instead, you investigate all its orifices to make sure it didn't bring in any hitchhikers before spraying it clean. It watches you from the stairs while you crush all the flushed snails with your boot.

After that, you polish it with a rag and cart it into your room. You heave it onto the spare twin bed across from you. The bare mattress creaks under the weight of two yous. *Dud,* you think, feeling your lookalike's corn silk hair and rind-hard ankles and wrists. This other self never ripened. There may be a pocket of flesh or two languishing in its core, but realization was out of the question before you picked it.

You drape a towel over its underdeveloped chest. Seeing yourself exposed without baggy clothes brings discomfort. Then you dig out your shortbread tin of weed and head downstairs to the phone.

The curls of the phone wire hang thick with dust as you dial up one of your cousins again. All the ancient almanac calendars, lopsided furniture, and dessicated seed packets magnet-pinned to the fridge haven't shifted a centimeter since you were five years old. They disintegrate in place.

The pin-up posters streaking the walls with painted tits and thighs are yours, as is the dart board, but they retain a dried quality. You hung them before you left. Nothing has swayed them since. You light a joint as the call rolls to the answering machine.

"Hey, asshole," you say, jabbing an entry in the withered contact book, "I found a huge lookalike behind the house today. Christ knows how that thing isn't ripe. We're lucky it was a bad crop. What's wrong with y'all? No one has done jackshit to keep the garden in shape. One of you has gotta help me. Call me back. I mean it."

You hang up, exhale a cloud, then punch in the next series of numbers in the phone book. Five disconnected numbers in, you ash your joint. No one's personal information is current. Come to think of it, do you know where any of your fifteen cousins live anymore?

You chew on the roach, highly heartsick, when you dial Frankie Harnell's number for good measure. Each time, the call goes through before clicking off.

This story originally appeared in *Strange Weeds: A Charity Anthology,* September 2022.

After three dials you put your head on the table.

■

You're checking out the items for a fried thirty-something with a baby on her waist and a curl of perm foil in her up-do, shoveling cups of cling peaches, diaper packages, and nicotine patches into plastic bags, when your shitty coworkers start arguing about the National Enquirer headlines. The one with long hair shoots you a sneaky glance.

"I don't know nothing about how a flying saucer works," he says, "but I bet Mister Community College over here could explain it to us."

"I didn't get an associate's degree in flying saucers," you say.

"Course not." He nods at you. "You spent two years getting one in..."

"Welding."

The thirty-something jitters her leg and flips through the personal ads. You ignore her turnipesque baby.

"Must not be too many welding jobs outside of Piper's Gap," Long Hair says.

"Reckon not."

"That's a shame, since you've got the degree and everything."

"Yeah."

"My mom's looking for a welder." Glasses Boy chimes in from the side. Long Hair grins as you punch open the cash register and give the thirty-something her change.

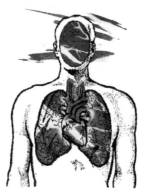

"I'll talk to your mom later," you say, longing to spit *when she's blowing me* but too scared of what the grocery goons will discuss if you do. The baby shrieks.

Long Hair almost snickers.

■

From where you sit in your room, you can see out your window to the dark, new pavement on the road. It's almost hidden by the waist-deep grass that rustles around your house.

"That road used to be full of potholes," you inform your lookalike, loading a bowl. "You can drive on it without killing your suspension now. I don't know when that happened. I don't know when anyone got the money to do that."

Your lookalike doesn't flinch when you blow a bong rip at them. You study the curves of its distorted body — the Woodward body. The lookalike's nudity is natural. It's like purveying a squash in a bowl. You're unsure why your own body seems so rotten and wrong. It's not uglier than your lookalike.

The clipped umbilical cord has become a stem. It protrudes from the lookalike's navel, horn-like. A vine ringlet hangs from its top and drapes onto the lookalike's pelvis. You don't touch your lookalike's ripe stretches until you've smoked your bowl. With your mouth dry and fingers tingling, you stroke your lookalike's ribs.

The skin is fuzzy. Room temperature. You stroke the ribs again before reaching for the face. Parts are unripe, here, hard and malformed. The nose is sunken, the cartilage green. You pet the dandelion fluff eyebrows before rolling the lookalike's lip up under your thumb. As expected, empty gums greet you. A handful of pumpkin seed teeth protrude in the front. You don't need to pluck one to know they're rubbery.

"You're as ugly as some of the little bastards outside," you say.

The lookalike sits unmoving in its dented spiderweb. You set your bong down and lean in. No breath brushes your cheeks. The lashes smell of lavender. You rip them out in clumps and pack them into your bowl.

"We're stuck." You watch the grass sway outside. "You're us, but worse. I'm me. There ain't much either of us can do."

When you're relaxed, you jam a jar between your lookalike's stiff thighs, then feed the umbilical into its aspirin-laced water. No point in letting it rot early.

■

"Lord, you're one of the Woodwards, aren't you?"

The old man with glasses thicker than spit squints. His arthritic claws stay clamped around his coupons. You scan his newspaper, denture cleaner, and ginseng pills.

"Guilty as charged," you say. "I'm the tenth one."

The old man waves. "The tenth one? Christ almighty. Half the town's a Woodward. 'Til recently, none of 'em left Piper's Gap through nothing but the courthouse."

Your teeth grind.

"I've been out," you say. "Went to community

college and everything. I almost moved to Clifton Forge, after I graduated, but the trailer —"

"You've all got the same look about you," the old man says. "All you Woodwards. Lots of funky teeth and fine, fine hair. You're all cousins too, ain'tcha? I've never seen a Woodward senior."

"Yeah." His receipt rips in your grip. "We are."

The old man's daughter, a middle-aged bruiser that's more piercings than skin, raps on the window, her truck idling. "Come on," she mouths. He gives you a paternal warning look.

"Be good, now," the old man says. "M'am. Sir. Whichever one. That don't matter. A Woodward is a Woodward."

Go fuck yourself.

You smile. "Have a nice day."

■

While you ponder where the old waterpark went and when the library moved, you prune the garden. Most families have a tree. Yours has a vine. You crawl beneath the noon sun, taking stock of what grows on the vine's winding, greedy tendrils. The ragged leaves. The tissuey blossoms. The embryonic scallop squashes. Green filigree ensnares the yard, pulsing with sickly life.

You stand there at the root of your family's genesis, two shoplifted fudgesicles chilling your guts, an electricity bill chilling your heart, thistle stings burning your hands. Disgruntlement sets in. You don't know when cultivating the next generation became a chore. The tasks haven't changed, but all awe has fled. The lookalikes are annoying vegetables; maintaining the Woodward vine means nothing but weeding and spreading cow shit around.

No wonder everyone dumped this on me, you think. *No one enjoys nasty work.*

Two of the embryonic squashes, no bigger than your fist, fared poorly last night. One's head was eaten halfway through by a deer. Another's punctured belly swarms with beetles. Their bulging eyes are knots, their mouths deadend indentations. They gnarl into themselves as they dangle from the vine. It's too early for their pseudo-fetal shapes to have Woodward features. In several months, they would have begun manifesting.

You snap the embryos free, chop them in half, and hurl them into a bucket, pitted innards and all. Lookalikes don't suffer. You can't empathize with that anymore. Realization means agony. Even if lookalikes

Their bulging eyes are knots, their mouths deadend indentations. They gnarl into themselves as they dangle from the vine.

did feel pain, the town doesn't want more Woodwards. Your selectivity does everyone a favor.

God knows your cousins don't do favors anymore. All this is on you.

You soak rags in your lookalike's damp mouth to replace the fly strips you can't afford as you dial your unresponsive family again, crying out more than greeting them, even when confused strangers answer your calls that go through.

■

"Mom says you haven't asked her about the job yet," Glasses Boy says.

"Blow me."

You slash at another pile of boxes with your box cutter. The stench of weed wafts into your hoodie. Glasses Boy smirks. Helpless rage makes your peripheral vision a mirage.

"Pretty sure that won't teach you how to weld," Glasses Boy says. "Think you participated in enough blow jobs the last two years anyhow, depending on where they put you."

"I'm going to the register," you mutter. "You can handle all this."

"You sure you want to, smelling like that? If the sheriff comes back in here again it'd be bad news."

It's impossible to tell if concern or mockery glitters in Glasses Boy's expression. You tear into another box. Soon enough, you're alone in the backroom.

■

"You're a fuck-up," you hiss at the vegetable in your room, grinding your spliff into its wrist again. "You know that?"

The lit end sizzles against the lookalike's peel. It leaves a fifth blistered circle. Its newly zip-tied wrists glow with charred spots. Despite all the crushed aspirin and water changes, the lookalike is rotting. Fingernails lengthen as its skin recedes; its hair mimics growth as its scalp shrinks. The zip ties cuffing the lookalike's ankles peer half-visible from their canals in the skin. Flies crawl on your sweating wallpaper.

"You never get anything right." You can't choose between fuming or crying. "Fucking hell."

You opt to rekindle your spliff's cherry with another puff and jab again.

When you stumble out back, spent, you sink to your knees among the family vine. Its latticework of purple veins throb with sap. You see double the veins and double the hungry, reaching leaves as your vision comes undone. Slugs, remembering past meals, slither towards you before turning away. Katydids stumble through your leg hair.

I want a machete, you think. Then: *Why?* What would you do with it? Ridding yourself of this legacy, somehow, is as unfathomable as quitting your job.

You sit outside until cricketsong calls the dark home.

■

The rat-tail adorned creep in a hoodie scratches at his mustache, if that waterline mark of hair can be called a mustache. You ring up the third bottle of robitussin he's come in to buy this week instead of making eye contact. His gaze burns into your name tag as you bag a bottle of lube, mentos, and a whipped cream canister.

"Hey!" he says. "I used to see you around here."

You grunt. "I've worked here a long time."

"Didn't you work with Frankie at that sheet cake place?"

Bile splashes up into your throat.

"No," you say. "I'm Frankie's best friend. Have been since ninth grade."

"Huh. I mean, I saw you two together all the time, but Frankie looked grouchy, and you don't really lounge around a cake place 24/7 'less you've got a reason to be there. So I assumed—"

"Frankie has a resting bitch face," you say.

"I don't think so." The creep frowns. "Her resting face looks pretty bored. At least before she sees me."

You want to strangle him. Your self doubt leashes you. "Your total is $15.75," you say. "Anything else?"

The creep wipes his runny nose. "If you didn't get put away for something violent, and that big ole hoodie isn't too loose on you uptop, I, uh, need your number."

"Go back to doing whippets in study hall, asshole," you say.

The creep pays in sweaty bills and coins before slinking out the door. Your coworkers burst into laughter. You rip apart the creep's receipt, boiling. You wish Frankie Hartnell was here to defend the mutuality of your friendship. You aren't sure she would. Did all that borrowed money and bummed rides to school mean friendship, or was that just proximity? Frankie didn't live far from you. Her family hired yours for odd jobs. Maybe obligation is proximity's neighbor. While you're restocking milk, you try to imagine Frankie's resting expression. Nothing but blurred features clutter your brain.

You know even less about your best friend than you know about yourself.

■

One of the older propagations who's ghosting you said *You are what you imbibe.*

He was smart, in the ubiquitous Woodward way. Still is, unless you've missed another death. You bet your fillings he escaped Piper's Gap after you. Maybe he tricked some middle class girl into marriage. That would be a hard sell, since none of you have the equipment for spousal duties or creating children, but Woodwards excel at rooting in hostile ground.

Your cousin meant his comment in the sense of flesh consuming flesh, of what separates lookalikes and people, but you hope that consuming yourself will get you closer to who you are.

You lean over your lookalike as you flick open your box cutter. The fact this botanic miscarriage shifts at night while it sinks into the mattress means your time is limited. Soon, it'll be fertilizer.

The blade shakes when you puncture the lookalike's side. There's a pop. At once, your tension flees. It feels no different than cutting a zucchini. You slice a square into the lookalike's unmoving abdomen, fumble, then peel the pane of skin free.

The skin unsuckers from the body. The muscle underneath is the color and texture of milkweed stem: white, wet. Seepage comes, but no blood. Your lip curls as you set the peel aside to dry for rolling paper.

Every day, you remember this thing isn't fully realized. You aren't either, but you're made of named meat, which puts you damn well above this gourd. It pays no rent; it wears no worries. It reclines in decaying repose at your mercy and burdens you.

"You could've been worth something," you tell it, knowing it cannot hear you crying in your adjacent twin bed at night. "Not anymore."

Its lashless eyes stare ceilingward, its bound wrists making its posture meek.

■

Mrs. Pryor has three bottles of black hair dye, migraine medication, and one apple in her basket. You're so sick with joy to see her that you overlook Glasses Boy ringing up Frankie Hartnell an aisle over. Not that Frankie or Mrs. Pryor is too close to you.

"Mrs. Pryor!" you say. "Long time no see!"

She starts. Her eyes are watery. The tote she's slotted into the bag carousel wilts. Mrs. Pryor always looked unsteady compared to her volleyball-spiking daughter. She looks ready to collapse now.

"Goodness," she says. "Is that who I think it is?"

"In the flesh." You vibrate. "How are you? How's Abilene? I haven't seen her since graduation! Did she end up moving to Blacksburg after she got her savings back up? I know her car brakes kept giving her trouble."

Mrs. Pryor's bistre skin turns ashen. She wavers.

"Abilene died last year, dear," she says. "We sent you an invitation to the funeral."

You stare at the quivering woman in front of you. Your guts may as well be on the conveyor belt. Asking what happened is futile.

"Sorry," you say. "I didn't get it."

"We sent it to your apartment address."

"I wasn't living there for too long."

Mrs. Pryor's hands worry at her bonnet. No wedding band gleams her on fingers now. You doubt her ring would fit without adjustment anyway. She's dropped four sizes in everything.

"You're the last Woodward left in these parts. What have you been doing with your life, honey," she says, "now that everyone up and left?"

You can't tell if that's a question for you or herself.

"I don't know," you say.

The migraine medication clatters in its box. Mrs. Pryor flees without waiting for her change. You stumble to the break room to hold your head in your hands.

∎

That Sunday night when you break down, you locate none of your fifteen cousin-siblings in the county phone book, or forwarding addresses, or married names, or anything, which is why you end up tearing one of your lookalike's hands free from the zip-ties and crawling beneath its disgustingly pliable arm, baked and bawling.

"I'm sorry," you tell it, dripping ash onto its collarbone with your joint while you sob into its cloying neck. "I've done you dirty. You're a shitty rotting vegetable but you're all I've got. No one else is here. No one else wants to be here."

The lookalike's pupils twitch. Your heart clenches. You cry out.

It can't be alive. It wasn't on the vine long enough, your rational brain says. The rest of you screams, *It's alive enough to know what you're doing.* How else could it move?

You straddle the lookalike. The sap congealing on the milkweed muscle sticks to your knee. The graffiti you carved into its waist yesterday scratches you. The lengthened, decomposing umbilical wilts beneath your weight. A splash of water from the jar splatters the lookalike's thighs.

"Here."

You're blubbering as you tilt its jaw up. Saline drowns your vision. You nearly cough to death on your first drag before you puke spit onto the hardwood. You sniffle, finish gurgling, then wipe your face. Your vision is no better than before.

"I'll give you a treat," you say. "You're gonna be compost anyway. Sorry. Here, here."

You take a deep pull of the joint. The lookalike's mouth opens with a moist click when you jam your fingers into the sides and squeeze. You lean in. The clack of its teeth against yours startles you. Your exhale of weed smoke vanishes into the lookalike's throat. Instead of bouncing back, it flows into sinus chambers connected to somewhere.

You hear squirming.

With the sound of an overripe melon splitting, the back of the lookalike's head bursts open. It spills forth seeds, dreamsicle pulp, and the true movers in the lookalike's rotting shell: a sea of white, writhing worms.

When you're done screaming, you sweep the worms into a grocery bag. Tear out the hair that has gunk entwined in it. Tie the bag. Cover the lookalike with a tarp. Crawl into bed, sniffling, angrily alone. You don't have the heart to drag that overgrown buffet out back tonight.

∎

You're fiddling with your radio, tuning it to the country station you like, one foot on the bike pedal, when you see her coming up the sidewalk. Frankie Hartnell has bad highlights and a blown-out butterfly tattooed on her stomach now, but she's the same glorious bitch she was in high school.

"Don't get off your bike." Frankie guards her growing belly with a palm. Her two broken french tips gleam against the butterfly's wings.

"Frankie," you say, weak. "Jesus Christ. It's been forever. What's going on?"

Frankie's exhale misses several stairs on its way down to you. Her gummy vitamins, batteries, and kitschy bibs rattle in her grocery bag.

"Can't you check a newspaper to get caught up?" she says. "Fuck. Stop calling me. My boytoy works the night shift. I've had to keep the phone off the hook so you don't wake him up."

"I want to hear from my best friend."

You feel as misshapen and inarticulate as your lookalike. Frankie's frown overflows with pity. She fiddles with her clutch.

"I don't know how to tell you this," she says, "but

being your only friend ain't something that makes me your best one. Not on my end. Please let this go, for your sake and mine."

"Everything's up and changed." You don't know why you're pleading, or what you're pleading for, but you want there to be some kind of truth living in all the space in your clothes and lungs. "I ain't heard shit from anyone. Abilene's dead. Did you know that Abilene was dead?"

"Abby and I hadn't talked for a year before she died," Frankie says. "I imagine there's a reason your own cousins aren't talking to you either."

"Look, I didn't hurt no one," you say. "That's not why I did time. But everyone treats me like a leper. Frankie, I can't keep paying bills or handling family business with the job I'm working. You've gotta know if another place will hire me."

"I am sorry, y'know." Frankie forges on. "But I'm barely staying afloat myself."

A singer croons about killing women in the gap that tears open between the two of you. The urge to swing builds in your fists, outstripped by the urge to cry. You can't swing at Frankie now. It wouldn't be a fair fight.

"Good luck." Frankie rubs her temple. "Honest."

"I don't want luck," you say. "I want *help*."

"Pray," Frankie suggests, as she climbs into her death trap of an ancient jeep.

It sounds a lot like 'drown.'

∎

Dusk falls into something darker as you bike towards your trailer. You're the sort of homesick that includes your body too, so you spent hours biking around downtown, hoping to find recognition here as you avoided your family plot. You found nothing. None of the whitewashed storefronts are as they were, none of the people the same. How has the world changed so much in two years? Whatever you've lost, there's no way to get it back.

You hunch over your grainy radio. Grass swats your legs, whispering. Charley Pride comes in and out of static, singing of snakes crawling at night. Castor and Pollux are above you with all the sneakers caught in telephone lines.

It takes a moment to realize the trailer door is a black, open rectangle.

It takes another to realize someone is in the driveway.

Gravel spins. Your bike stops. You stare at the gnarled, naked figure twelve feet in front of you. Their face is not in the light. You make out the pale square of muscle well enough. The zip-tie hanging from a leaking wrist. Bleeding graffiti. Here and there, a worm falls through the flashlight beam. You cannot tell who moves when the flashlight begins flickering.

As it gives out, you hear the crunch of feet on gravel. A horrible peace germinates within you. Freedom is coming. In a sense.

Sometimes, you imagine, the self wants to taste back.

Samir Sirk Morató is a scientist, artist, and flesh heap. Some of their published and forthcoming work can be found in Flash Fiction Online, X-R-A-Y, ergot., NIGHTMARE, *and* The Drabblecast. *They are on Twitter and Instagram @spicycloaca.*

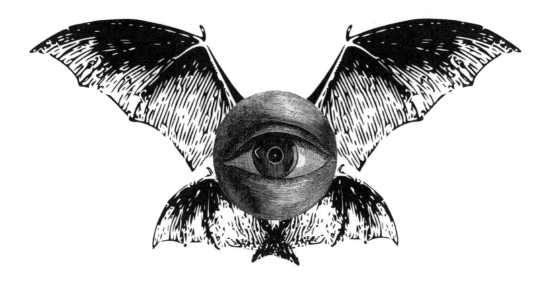

Variations on the Memory Palace

By AVRA MARGARITI

THE STORIES WILL GET IT WRONG LATER: I was trapped in my head long before I was trapped in this house.

.

Mom is showing the cancer wall to the exorcist. Her bald hair shines in the low-light of the oil lamps flickering under each family portrait: grandmother, great-aunt, cousin, aunt. All severe-looking in their gilded frames, all dead within years of each other; hair shed in thin clumps, muscles wasted away, eyes candescent with illness and a futile will to hold on.

My body hugs the corner of the corridor — though sometimes it's hard to tell where my physical body is located when I dissociate hard enough to sink into the unreal architecture of my memory palace. As I listen to Mom drone on about our dead relatives and our cells' curse, I realize I know this exorcist my family has summoned.

Annamaria or Annalisa or some similar synergy of family names. I try to access the smart-house's infostream, but if the exorcist has a neural implant, it's safeguarded from unauthorized probing. We weren't classmates, but the exorcist was a couple of grades higher than me in school. One of those girls people always whispered one day would slip between the cracks of the world and disappear. And yet the exorcist is here in our house, more present than I am. I keep floating away and within — not dead, but a noetic ghost in the making.

This is why my mother has hired the exorcist. She believes the house to be haunted by one of our many dead, causing the AI interface to malfunction: heated floors burning hapless feet, smart-doors slamming on careless fingers, music briefly deafening unsuspecting ears. She doesn't know my submersions into my warped inner world are to blame for all these strange phenomena occurring around the house.

The exorcist is patient. She doesn't rush Mom when she talks about all the types of cancer, failed treatments, numerous tombstones. When Mom's nervous hand smooths over her naked scalp, the exorcist's eyes follow the trajectory. She doesn't ask if Mom is the only one so far to survive. Cancers are wriggly things. Like insect infestations, they keep coming back once you think you've rid your house of them.

I remember the cancer wall well. I was brought in front of it before Mom's first diagnosis. Mom's fingers digging into my younger-self's shoulder, her head lustrous with long, brown curls as she said, "This will never be you, I promise you."

In my mind palace, the cancer wall is swathed in amorphous mist. Each portrait displays a corrupted organ squirting black juice between cracks in necrotic tissue. The last frame bears a face smooth and white and featureless. Only two blank eyes emerge, like someone pushed thumbs into clay to make indistinct divots. I can't tell if that last face belongs to me, or to my mother.

Mom turns back to the exorcist, her fingers caressing the wainscoting's peeling wood. "The house groans, doesn't it? Like it's hurting. Like it's in pain."

Mom doesn't know that my memory palace resembles our house but inverted, all the rooms and their hidden crannies remade strange and monstrous, hallways paved with jagged fragments of my own mind and body.

That the haunting is no ghost's fault, but my own.

When the exorcist bends down to dig into her suitcase for supplies, she locks gazes with me from across the corridor. It feels like the house has been caught in perpetual twilight ever since the haunting started. No luminescence penetrates the corridor where the portraits hang, dull brushstrokes masking the wear of illness.

Her brown eyes widen. "Oh, hey, I know you. We went to school together. You're —"

But I've already vanished back inside my head, not knowing what my body says to the exorcist in response.

.

Today's room is a giant fig. I enter through the ostiole, fleshy thalamus enfolding me, wasps buzzing all around. I lick the walls for their nectar, the pulpy red seeds and purple grain. The fig devours me in return, because I too am a wasp, another infestation like the cancer cells in my mother's body.

Within this noetic pocket, I coagulate like fat left on the stove. I buzz like an angry thing. I feel my body being broken down and subsumed, mellified into its key components.

A sound. Someone's intruding on my memory palace and the giant fig that mirrors the placement of the house's dining room. I can hear the exorcist's inscrutable devices scraping against the syconium wall. Is she trying to use a dowsing rod to pinpoint the rot of this house, the root of its so-called ghosts? Are her methods nanites and algorithms, or sea-salt and spellwork?

I curl up smaller in my tight cocoon, wrapping membranous wings around my resinous body. The fig's guts cradle me like my mother's body once did, sparing me from illness, from harm. Among sticky sap, I try to make myself invisible, the way I have for all twenty years of my life. My family never notices when I disappear into the mind palace. So why would the exorcist?

She hums as she works on the other side of the syconium, across parallel planes of reality. I let myself be lulled to near-sleep by her voice — a mistake.

When the exorcist's hand penetrates the wall of the dining room, the fruit-skin doesn't break, but stretches to accommodate her. Her palm is silhouetted in viscous fig guts.

Heart drumbeating, I scramble away from the intrusion, resurfacing before the exorcist can peek inside my soul.

•

The next day, in the brown-dressed sitting room, I catch my brother trying to flirt with the exorcist. They were in the same grade in school, both three years older than me. I peek, half-hidden behind the doorframe, ears strained to catch their exchange. I log into the house's network as well, accessing my brother's vitals.

"Didn't you use to sell your worn underwear in high school?" my brother asks the exorcist, leaning into her space.

I want to call out his behavior, the kind Mom and Dad always excused as him being young, being stupid, being boy.

But the exorcist squares her jaw and shoulders, and holds her own. "Have you noticed any ghostly activity around the house? What about the strange phenomena your mother talks about?"

The rapidly changing temperatures and cracking walls, she means. The groans traveling through the intercoms like another cancer through the house's AI interface. The burglar alert that keeps mistakenly summoning the police, no matter how many times Dad's called the tech people over to check for bugs and data-leaks.

"Sure," my brother says, beckoning the exorcist closer to his sharp-edged smirk. "Sometimes my laptop randomly plays porn with the volume up. And wouldn't you know, sometimes the porn actresses resemble you!"

The exorcist scoffs. Yet she goes on ignoring him, like she's used to dealing with people like him. In school she was a tomboy, a tomcat spitting and fighting. Once, I'd found her tent, where she'd been sleeping rough in the thicket of trees behind the tennis courts. She swore me to secrecy, and I complied. Though I know now I should have done more to help her, despite her being wiser, tougher, older than me.

The exorcist says, "I cannot feel any spirits in this house. But I feel *something*. I just need to figure out the root of the disturbance."

I must make a sound at the prospect of being discovered, my memory palace — the only safe retreat to call my own — potentially breached. Inside my

inner architecture, Mom cannot cry about me as if I'm already dead, nor can I worry about her cancer metastasizing. I don't have to be a good, sweet daughter for my poor overworked Dad. Nor do I need to avoid my brother's slurs and gross behavior.

Before I turn to leave, I catch my brother's eyes — something almost akin to regret flashes in this boy with the dead or dying family members who never taught him accountability. His heartbeat spikes red through the house's infostream feedback.

The exorcist has turned in my direction as well. She says, "Hey, it's you —"

■

I dive into the old music box that lives on my bedroom's nightstand, but also inside my head. Another echoing chamber of my memory palace, replete with cavernous, etched wooden walls and a marble platform for me to dance on. I twirl round and round, trapped in place inside the ballerina costume my mother bought for me back when she was trying to make me more graceful. More feminine.

Whenever I am hurt, a new room materializes in the memory palace. These are the mirror-image hallways I can wander for hours, immortalizing the hurt with each footfall that ghost-echoes up into my family's house. When my brother once called me a fat lesbian, my palace built itself a hidden cupboard filled with flabby flesh writhing in masturbating spurts. The music box is the manifestation of my mother's hopes for me. In it, I am a pink slip of a thing, becoming more starved, more twiglike with each pirouette. In my tattered tutu, I dance to outrun the illness that stole one life per generation. The ballerina box is lined with torn up paper: the genetic testing that predicted my chances of developing cancer. Words peek through the paper scraps —

Breast, marrow, lung, brain.

My pain oozes miasmic through the thin membrane between real and unreal architecture. It makes the physical house desperate enough to bite pieces off its dwellers, to devour.

As if summoned by my haunting, she appears.

The exorcist leans over the music box on my bedroom's nightstand. She appears large and looming from my vantage point, a giant. Her eyes are brown flecked in honey. The pores of her nose like craters deep enough for me to nest in.

Inside the music box, a memory: when I first found the exorcist was a runaway, she had offered me a kiss in exchange for keeping her secret. I refused, though my disgust was aimed toward the

people requiring a bribe to keep her safe in the past. But the prospect of kissing her, touching her … No, it was not disgust I felt at that fantasy.

I watch the exorcist's hand move toward the dancing ballerina figurine that resembles me. Her touch lands upon my tutu, a musical dissonance as the mechanism halts, a discordant screech as the exorcist is propelled out of my memory palace with a yelp of pain.

■

Dad is in the kitchen, preparing tea from cheap bags for the exorcist. No matter the wealth my family acquires, he always buys the cheap ones. His hands tremble as he mixes sugar like cancerous lumps at the bottom of the chipped mug. The sunny stream of chatter expelled out of his mouth doesn't match his eyes or the kitchen's aphotic, oppressive atmosphere.

"Sir," the exorcist says. She's at the table, jittery as if she's not used to sitting still, or being invited to tea, no matter how lukewarm and weak. "Your wife seems to think the house is suffering from a ghost affliction, but none of my readings have detected any paranormal activity."

She taps at the screen of her tablet, projecting a holographic model of atmospheric pressure data, temperature, infrasound, air particle-sequencing. Lurking behind the door, I use the network's camera to peek at all her measurements, procured through bizarre tools and days of studying each room in the house. I wonder if her sensory readings can locate my memory palace. Can this fantasy-rot inside me be cartographed in 3D outside my head?

Dad is still muttering to himself, unable to engage with the exorcist's words. "I just can't lose my girls," he says into the teacup. His movements stutter for a moment, like an automaton. Then, he seems to shake himself. Through my own infostream readings, I know he is sweating profusely. "I mean, with so much illness running in the family, and now the ghosts, too. The ceiling cried tears of blood all day yesterday after you were gone."

I was there. The floor, too, undulated under my family's feet, the house trying to fell them like trees in a storm.

"That's the thing," the exorcist says, swallowing her frustration. I remember how she always liked solving a good puzzle in school. She was, after all, an A-student getting Fs for bad behavior. "It's not ghosts I sense. But there's definitely an electromagnetic disturbance. The house's network — it's the newest AI model, isn't it? A semi-sentient home-safety mechanism?"

Dad freezes. I do, too. "You think our hauntings have to do with the house network?"

The exorcist looks around her, as if she can see the invisible lines of code traversing the house like a mycorrhizal network of data meant to optimize a smart home, a safe home. "Sometimes technology creates echoes. Not exactly ghosts, but close. Digital alienation auras. Wi-Fi wraiths. I've seen it happen before."

Dad, wincing in pain, turns to look at me in the doorway, and the exorcist follows his trajectory.

"Hey, don't run away again, we need to talk!" she calls out.

Startled, Dad drops the exorcist's tea mug, now a brown puddle of liquid and porcelain shards staining the kitchen floor.

I run. I can't help it — all I know is how to retreat inside myself.

Yet this time, I know she will follow. And perhaps, I leave the door open just a crack.

.

"Do you know what a Fata Morgana is?" I ask the exorcist.

We are inside the Angel Room. She cannot see me, but the disembodied wings speak to her from open stomata gouged through their pinion feathers. I wonder if she will touch them, but she doesn't.

By this point, my memory palace is a labyrinthine structure. The exorcist doesn't have her fancy tools here. She would never find her way out if she found herself trapped. In our labyrinth, I would be the monstrous Minotaur and she, Ariadne with her thread cut to shreds.

"Like Morgan le Fay?" the exorcist asks after some hesitation. "The Arthurian enchantress?"

I love her a little for asking this. She is a mythology nerd turned ghost hunter. A broken child helping the broken. But there's no helping me.

"Yes. But also, the optical illusion." I swallow down a lump. "A Fata Morgana is a mirage."

The numerous pairs of wings shudder as I say this. I don't remember when the Angel Room first appeared in my ever-shifting landscape, but first there was a single pair, excised and pinned to the walls with nails through the blood-feathers. The original wings resembled organs grown too tumorous for their host. Now there are more: some big and some small. Some brown-speckled like

peregrine feathers, others the rainbow polyphony of parrots. Those last ones especially are covered in tar, blackened and smothered so their kaleidoscopic truth won't come out and lead to more pain. The oil-slicked parrot wings materialized after Dad sat me down and gently told me to forget all my bright ideas of confused teenage homoeroticism; we wouldn't want my poor, sick mom to get sicker with worry for me and my future, would we?

"Tell me about this illusion of yours," the exorcist says. She must be scared, surrounded by all these disembodied, dissected wings. To her credit, her voice doesn't waver. I have all the power here, but it doesn't make me feel any stronger.

So I tell her about the summer me and my family rented a cabin along the beach. How there was an illusion of sunrays and thermal inversion if you looked out at the sea-blued horizon: an inverted palace scintillating along the skyline, as if conjured by fay magic. This is what my memory palace is like, I tell her. I have taken the house I grew up in and cast its evil mirror twin, and now the runoff of my

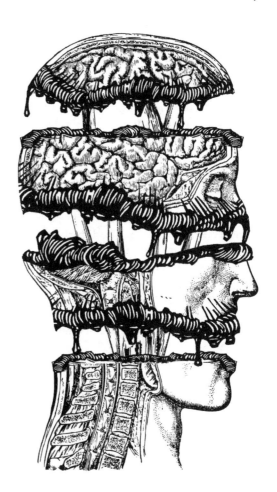

reality-shift has seeped into the house, corrupting it like a liminal glitch.

The angel wings are bleeding by the time I've finished the story. The stomata have become eyes shedding watery pink excretions.

"I'm sorry," the exorcist says. Like the wings, she is also crying. "This place, it can't be healthy for you."

"I've always had my memory palace," I reply. My voice ruffles the feathers, breezes over her wet cheeks.

She shakes her head. "The physical house, I mean. There is a miasma, and it's all directed toward you. Like the house itself wants to swallow you. I still don't know why, but I will get to the core of this, I promise. In the meantime, you should leave if you can. Whatever *it* is, we need to starve it, and currently you're its sole food source."

"I can't leave," I reply through a melancholy susur-rus of wings.

In the far corner of the Angel Room, the apparition of my mother is brandishing a rusty hand saw. She straps me down to a hospital gurney, spreads my tumorous wings out, saying, *I will excise the cancer in you, darling, I will make you safe, make you clean.* Yet, in the process, she also cuts away everything that is *me.* My mother, the lepi-dopterist, pins her newest butterfly specimen — an-other pair of wings nailed to the bleeding walls.

"You can," the exorcist says, vehement. "I did."

I think about finding the exorcist's makeshift campsite a few years ago. The food she stole from the school cafeteria to survive. The dirty clothes she sold to dirtier men for money. All to escape her own house haunted by family ghosts.

"You can, you are free. I'll help you," the exorcist says. I wonder if she thinks there is a debt she must repay. "We can leave together —"

But the angel mouths and eyes and wings are screaming.

The door I had left ajar for her slams in the exorcist's face.

∎

All my family members gather in the living room, past the looming cancer wall, bathed in perpetual crepuscule. Mom and Dad sit on the couch with my brother reluctantly in the middle, while I hover beside them. I am unable to meet the exorcist's

Like mycelium filaments, I travel through the neural network, witnessing the exchange from all angles.

eyes as she stands like a disgruntled general pacing before her unruly troops.

Her eyes linger on the bump of Mom's shiny-bald scalp, where last night a book fell on her head while the shelves shook with the anger of the house, or whatever lies within. Dad wears a lost expression on his too-pale, sunless face. My brother's sullen-ness belies his anxiety, but the infostream-collected biometrics rarely lie to me.

"I have finished mapping out the house," the exorcist announces with a tone of grave finality.

I wonder if she is about to give my secret away. Tell my family that it's my memory palace causing all this chaos. It's me, always a disappointment that can never do anything right. And suddenly, I see all the rooms in my palace like a series of tableaux, a montage of my being a bad daughter. The room where I was seated in front of a flickering old-film projector to be re-educated with my eyelids taped open, while in the real world, my family begged me to be normal, to fly under the radar and not cause them any grief. The room where toy soldiers played out toy wars of tiny viscera and rivulets of blood when I caught my brother posting on alt-right forums through the house's neural network. The times cancer lumbered like a monster through my memory palace, and my mother stroked my face, told me, *I am doing this to protect you, sit down, it will only hurt a moment and then you will be free —*

"I have completed my report, and your problem is not ghost related. But there still is a presence in the house. It's not an exorcist who can rid you of this problem. I suggest you move elsewhere until you figure out what's going on. The whole struc-ture — the bedrock, the brickwork, even the neural network — feels on the verge of collapse."

My family ignores the exorcist as she goes through her speech. My brother forces a laugh and winks at her, slow and out of tune. Mom mutters about the house hurting, *we cannot abandon it in its pain.* Dad says it was wrong of them to get an exorcist, *he always knew it wouldn't work.*

I say nothing. Hovering, buzzing with some-thing I cannot place.

The exorcist stands before me. *Anna-Maria,* her name, I remember now as I watch the honey flakes in her eyes without any filters or obstructions.

"Eleni," she says. She remembers my name, too. "Come outside with me."

"Where would we go?" I ask, flailing with loss.

She laughs and it's an ebullient sound. "Anywhere. On a stroll. For an ice cream."

For the kiss she once offered me and I couldn't accept back then.

I let my hand slip into hers. Let her lead me across the living room as my family calls my name with increasing agitation. All the way to the doorway, where the sunlight does not dare penetrate the murk of the house. In the threshold, I pause. I linger. Anna-Maria steps outside, our linked hands swinging in the liminal space between us. I look around the house, and the chambers of my memory palace superimposed upon it. The palace, I cannot escape; I built it myself brick by brick, and I don't know how to tear it down. But the house …

I take one step forward to meet Anna-Maria, only to be met with a cry of pain. A cry originating from within my throat. I look down at our linked hands, and mine is glitching, glorious technicolor slicing my jagged hands apart. I try and try, but I cannot seem to speak without stuttering, move without buffering, stop this terrible, grating glitch.

I cannot cross the threshold and meet my almost-savior in the sunlight.

■

The stories will get it wrong later. The house and I have always possessed each other equally.

■

Back inside the house, the exorcist is yelling while my mother gesticulates, at turns angry and beseeching as she tries to explain her point of view.

I am elsewhere, floating above and below and through every crack and quark of the house. Like mycelium filaments, I travel through the neural network, witnessing the exchange from all angles.

When I was in high school, we went on a museum trip to see a brain in a vat — wires stuck to neurons, connecting all to a supercomputer simulation. I wonder if the exorcist's class went on a similar trip. If she had the money for the admission fee.

"I told you," Mom shouts at the exorcist. "You stupid girl. I told you the house is in pain, but you wouldn't listen. I hired you to alleviate her pain, not take my only daughter away."

This won't hurt a bit, says the vista of my mother in my memory palace — no, my database of code and core memories running rampant in bytes and algorithmic sequences. Maneuvering my body into the machine, my mother says, *it's for your own good.*

So the cancer never finds you like it found me. I will hide you. You will never be a part of the cancer wall.

Yet I am still part of the wall, because I am part of the house. I am inside it, my body stasis-trapped in the basement's crawlspace, my monitored brain activity disseminated throughout everything. I rattle the cancer wall until the portraits fall and break like the bodies they depict once did in the real world. I turn the lights on and off. I access my brother's vile search history. I detect the rapid pulse of my father, the blood cell count of my mother. I corrupt, I corrupt, I am corrupted.

I am the house.

From a distance, through my multitude of sensors, I hear Mom and the exorcist fight while Dad tries to play mediator and my brother looks on, blank with numbness.

"I don't understand," the exorcist is saying. "Is your daughter dead? Or dying of cancer? Is that why you uploaded her consciousness to the house's network? It's an illegal procedure, but if there was no other choice —"

"You're right, you do *not* understand," Mom vehemently replies. "I showed you the cancer wall. You know the fate of all the women of this family. Should I have condemned my only daughter to that? Let go of my little girl?"

Lie back down, this won't hurt a bit. But it did. Cells transmuting into code, breath to byte. My crawlspace-hidden body held in pulsating tubes and whirring machine parts my brother ordered from the deep web at Mom's behest. My mind floating everywhere at once, realistic holograms of myself projected in each room, algorithmic delusions of my own making shielding the truth from myself to preserve what little sanity I had left. Yet the truth still slipped through: little hauntings I didn't know how to squash down and control.

"You trapped her here," the exorcist utters, face twisted with the realization. "The cancer didn't kill you. How do you know it will kill her? She doesn't have it yet. Perhaps she never will. You trapped her here because you didn't want your daughter to grow up and change into someone you wouldn't recognize."

Mom is trying to hold the exorcist back, but she keeps pushing her away. Chemo has weakened my mother. I can see her body's functions fraying in real time, while the exorcist burns through my heat sensors with a candescent fury.

I know what she's thinking. *Queer daughter. Strange daughter. Of course her parents would want to change her.*

But I'm too far away to care about this now. There is only one thing that still matters.

I make the floor shift, leading the exorcist where I want her. My old self materializes into a realistic hologram. I run for the last time, expecting the exorcist to follow me through my memory palace made manifest in algorithmic VR. The exorcist chases me past the Angel Room, the music box, the fig syconium, and all the other little hauntings I can no longer control now that I have come unraveled. I need to fix this, or else all will be lost.

"Where are you taking me? Is there another way out?" the exorcist pants. And: "I'm sorry they did this to you."

I do not reply, only send my hologram running down the stairs to the basement. I lock my family inside the living room, so they cannot interfere with what needs to be done. My sensors inform me some extant part of myself is weeping. I take that part and compress it into a foggy blue marble, which I suspend inside another space-dark room inside me.

The exorcist at last has made it to the basement, with its floor hatch leading down into the bricked-in crawlspace. I order the hatch open for her, revealing my body in its glass coffin, so still and placid as I am kept alive-but-stagnant through its manifold machines.

"Oh," the exorcist says, coming nearer to me — no, my former body.

If this were a fairytale, she would lean forward and kiss me over my glass coffin. The kiss I still owe her from when we were younger. Nodes falling away, she would bring me to life. Would call for help through her devices — the devices she doesn't yet know I have deactivated. The exorcist would save me, carrying me out of the house weak and atrophied and disoriented, but blissfully free.

When her fingers hover over my cheek, I slam the hatch shut behind her. My hologram vanishes. I trap her and my old body in the crawlspace-darkness of whirring machines, and I pretend not to hear her screams when I send forth filament-tubes to join her body, keep her stagnant, suppressed.

It will hurt, but she knows this already.

Perhaps the reason my parents so easily uploaded me was because I had spent such a long time retreating into my memory palace, retreading familiar steps. The walls of my mind — the house — were already pliant. Perforable. The exorcist resists for the longest time, but eventually she, too, submits to the procedure.

When I upload her to my database, I don't let her roam free. Nor do I let her think she is real. In my memory palace, the former exorcist is sleeping curled inside another marble, and she is having the sweetest dream. I take the marble, hued poppy-red to my sky-blue, and I let our marbles orbit each other inside my secret sidereal room in perpetuity.

Then, I time a system rewrite protocol for myself. In thirty minutes, the week since the exorcist entered our lives will be deleted, stored into another chamber whose cybernetic coordinates will be locked away even from myself. My core memories will remain unchanged, the little cruelties, little denials, little hauntings that brick by brick make up who I am the way they once built the palace in my mind. I am my family's daughter. I'm never going to end up on the cancer wall. I'm the girl of this house. I am safe.

Safe from the knowledge that my family would do this to me without my permission.

Safe from leaving the house only to find my hardcoded memories deleted, until nothing of me is left.

Safe from ex-schoolmates and exorcists thinking they can save me.

∎

You are free. You can leave. We will go together.

∎

The stories I tell myself will always get it wrong.

Avra Margariti is a queer author, Greek sea monster, and Rhysling-nominated poet with a fondness for the dark and the darling. Avra's work haunts publications such as Strange Horizons, The Deadlands, F&SF, Podcastle, Asimov's, Vastarien, *and* Reckoning. *You can find Avra on twitter (@avramargariti).*

Breaking Bad Habits

Chasing Autonomy in Nunsploitation and Religious Horror

By MO MOSHATY

LET'S SET THE SCENE: a nun travels to Rome in search of dedicating herself to the church and service, and then hang on wait a minute, girl where'd that baby come from? New scene: a young woman travels to Rome, to be of service to the church-run orphanage, and then wait, hang on, girl where'd that baby come from?

The nuns are having a MOMENT in horror this year! And although we've got similar themes, one obvious through-line shines through (and no, it ain't the habit)-it's the lack of body autonomy. Female protagonists are usually subject to situations where their autonomy over their bodies is compromised. That pesky tree in *Evil Dead*, that horrific chainsaw scene in *Terrifier*, and let's not forget the horrors of mutilation in *Boxing Helena*. It's an acute pursuit of control. And what we've got here in films like *Immaculate* and *The First Omen* (and there'll be more stops on the tour) is that we're dealing with religious and patriarchal systems which are often used as environments where women's choices are heavily dictated by tradition and devilish agendas, albeit under the guise of faith. What makes impregnating non-consenting women so attractive to religious characters in horror films? Is the horror that nothing terrible is supposed to happen to you in a church (erm)? Is it that the devil is still at work even through religious figures? Or is it simply a metaphor for the lack of women's safety anywhere and that even if we lay down our lives in dedication and give up earthly pleasures, we're still in danger of being violated?

Perhaps it's all of the above. Nunsploitation and the religious horror genre have served us well over the years as a glimpse into how cleanliness and godliness continue to be miles apart and how the work toward thorough control over women and their humanity can drive men mad. We're so used to the Devil being born that we've forgotten the emotional, mental, and physical violations that usually come first.

Was it always so invasive? Not really. We started off really strong in film about the silliness of patriarchal control and the awful public admonishment of the mentally ill.

With 1922's *Häxan* by writer and director Benjamin Christensen, the documentary-style horror shows the "evils" of devil worship and paganism and the psychological coercion that can take place from religious figures. Devilish monsters impaling and swallowing women who dared turn their faces away from God. A strong metaphor not only for the practice of staying devout and virtuous, but also for the label of hysteria thrust upon women who, heaven forbid, had their own way of thinking, operating, and protecting their bodily autonomy. Christensen demonstrates that the true hysteria lay within the baseless beliefs in superstition leading to the witch-hunting era and the mistreatment and degradation of those with mental illness foolishly mistaken for witchcraft or possession.

These themes of obedience and control favor the patriarchal umbrella. "If man cannot punish you, God will punish you, if God cannot punish you, the Devil will ... and we'll help him." It clearly takes a village to keep a good woman down, and the hope for loss of human frailty, once the habit goes on, seems to exhaust the church's many constraints.

Nuns were initially perceived in horror films

as flawed creatures: seeking their ingrained human needs, unable to decipher devoutness from desire, and traumatized by their own wants. And it was always the men-folk who were going to save them from themselves because clearly, they were incapable.

Mother Joan of the Angels or *Matka Joanna od Aniołów,* Jerzy Kawalerowicz's 1961 portrayal of a nun's agony as she's trapped between the sexual desires lacing her potent dreams, her possible demonic possessionwreaking spiritual havoc, and her boundary-pushing against the prelatic rigidity of the church. Not even Father Suryan, the browbeating cleric who initially shuns her conflict, can save her. He doesn't understand how the thoughts of pleasure, self-inflicted or otherwise, haven't left her after dedicating herself so truly to the church, and this leads him to question his own faith. Taking this exercise in human frailty as an impossibility and a personal affront to the church, Father Suryan performs several exorcisms on Joan. Surely it must be the devil at work on her — a woman continuing to have needs, questions, urges? When all else fails, the good Father breaks a pretty serious commandment to "save" Joan from herself.

When you toss religious fanaticism on the fire, there's smoke ...

And no one had more smoke than Sister Ruth in Powell and Pressburger's *Black Narcissus* of 1947, based on the novel by Rumer Godden. A convent skulks atop the mountains of the Himalayas where the establishment of a school and hospital are in the midst of construction in an old palace. The isolated and harsh climate heaves a dark and heavy breath into the Anglican Sisters' domicile, and with that breath comes Mr. Dean, the agent of the Indian General who owns the building. Mr. Dean makes quite an impression on the nuns, sparking lust, want, jealousy, and competition, not to mention questioning all they are meant to believe in. Even though there's plenty of man-swooning, mean mugging, fierce lipstick, and attempted murder — surprisingly this film passes the Bechdel test. But it's a stark look at the psychological ramifications of caging and isolating women in the hopes that their human needs and wants will simply wash away if they're told to.

The toxicity of isolation and human weakness play heavily in 1979's *Killer Nun,* where Sister Gertrude, an ailing nun, returns after recovering from brain surgery. Upon her return, she

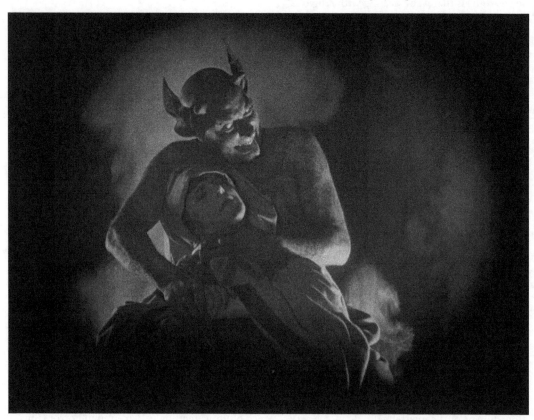

Benjamin Christensen as the Devil in *Häxan* (1922) • Public Domain

Clara Pontoppidan as Sister Cecilia in *Häxan* (1922) • Public Domain

can't shake the feeling of her cancer returning. Shrugged off by everyone but Sister Matthieu, her confidante and secret admirer, she spirals out of control. Slipping into the city and having casual sex with many partners and engaging in intravenous drug use. When folks around the convent begin dropping dead in the goriest of ways, she deems herself responsible — she's uncontrollable and on a murderous rampage. It's a bulletin on how not to be a nun but further speaks to the fallibility of religious figures and the cloak of secrecy and cover-ups that happen behind church doors, and the guilt and repression that I'm sure befalls every person who dedicates themselves so wholly to something that represses their human nature.

So where did the flip from isolation to pure violation come in? Most likely with the 1968 film adaptation of Ira Levin's novel *Rosemary's Baby*. It's a story for the ages, or I suppose, a tale as old as time. We open with sweet and unassuming Rosemary and Guy Woodhouse touring what will soon be their New York apartment at The Bramford. The previous tenant, having gone mad, has passed, leaving the apartment free to rent. Their new neighbors, the elderly, ever-creepy, and far too nosey Minnie and Roman Castevet cast a "spell" over Guy with the promise of fortune and fame if he promises to help them let the devil violate his wife. Guy jumps at the sweet deal and gets to work right away, opening the door for the Castevets to come over unannounced and invade as they please. Throw the entire husband away.

What's so incredibly isolating, still, is that Rosemary is gaslit from Day One. Horrible things, such as Guy hiding said violation under the guise of marital rape, witnessing suicides, having strange visions and terrifying thoughts, are all explained away. And even after giving birth to the Devil's child, Rosemary stoically accepts her fate. We've teetered into not only the violating religious horror but peppered in the hysterical woman trope, and even in the end, she's no further forward in placement than she was at the beginning. She's merely a prop, a vessel, and leaning into that is incredibly disheartening.

In the plainest terms, the crux of nunsploitation and religious horror always resides in the fanciful allure of childhood innocence, the patriarchal zealots who lust for it and the pick-me nuns that facilitate it. But why?

The patriarchal idea of "pureness" and compliance is in short supply these days — seemingly due to women owning their worth and stepping into self-reliance, apparently a big no-no. So the best means to an end is to drug, isolate, gaslight, impregnate, and watch the horrific magic happen, because truly, no one in their right mind would go along with these ridiculous plans. And as much as we put on nuns in our earlier era of films, so flawed and so frail, the tyrannical clergy seemed the most defective. Using a woman and her body to do the dirty work you're too ill-equipped or inept at speaks *volumes* in religious horror. These faulty Fathers carry much more of the guilt they project upon the women in these stories, and the gift of control is bestowed upon them when they follow through.

The male clergy in these texts and films always work to strike fear and complacency, and within the walls of the church they're working alongside the devil — which is the most "if you can't beat 'em, join 'em" energy I've ever heard of. Dedicating your entire life, livelihood, and mental space to an organization just to side with the competition is the look of an office temp who just won the lottery. Two middle fingers up — burn it all down, at the expense of innocent women of course. And burn they do …

Where 2024's *Immaculate* begins is like most religious horrors. An innocent arrives to dedicate themselves to the church. Naturally, you've got the ones that hate the new kid on the block, and the scruffy new best friend who helps her get adjusted. These are the playful tropes we expect. Where Sidney Sweeney's "Cecelia" goes wrong is snooping around the church to find all the creepy goings-on and pissing off Sister Isabelle, a rigid nun with a HUGE chip on her shoulder.

The First Omen begins in much the same fashion, a religious conspiracy chatted in secret and punished by a swift death, and here lands American novitiate Margaret Daino — played exquisitely by Nell Tiger Free — at an orphanage in Rome run by uber-cunty Cardinal Lawrence, and she later meets her free-spirited scruffy sidekick Luz, who takes her to a disco. Each woman takes a mildly different detour, but in both instances, these women are chosen and brought miles from home for the church's dirty dealings in much the same way — caught up in conspiracy, impregnated against their will, and left for dead all in the name of pleasing the Devil. Lather, rinse, repeat. A vessel is a vessel is a vessel. I wonder if the Devil is a vast metaphor for the patriarchy at large; if Regan MacNeil's childish form spoke to the lure of innocence; if Damien's nanny and the housekeeper had been men, would they be so easily possessed; if pick-me nuns didn't want the respect of their sullied cohorts, would there be fewer attempts at Devil-babydom. The wonders never cease. Choose the bear.

This consistent theme of women in nunsploitation and religious horror continues to act as an expression of women's pure lack of safety in most male-dominated spaces, in our lives, on a global scale, in text, and within film. Even in our dedication to churches of all dominations, in all our sacrifice, violence and demoralization will still find a way to pervade. The patriarchal structure is meant to maintain authority and subdue women's autonomy. Nunsploitation and religious horror are stark reminders of the inequities that have imbrued in our society and continue to torment women, and until these issues are addressed through movement, through law, and through behavior, they will prevail.

I hope that we can turn our frame away from the violation of women's bodies for sport in religious horror. Don't get me wrong kids, I'll honestly watch you fight the Devil all day, but I'm begging y'all — stop trying to make the Antichrist happen.

Mo Moshaty — Cognitive Behavioral Therapist and lifelong horror fan — has lectured with Prairie View A&M Film & TV Program as a Keynote, BAFSS Horror Studies Sig, and The University of Sheffield in the United Kingdom. Partnered with Shudder, Mo co-produced the 13 Minutes of Horror Film Festival 2021 and 2022.

"From Inside the House", Mo's new podcast under the Mourning Manor Media banner, will explore women's trauma within horror cinema. Each episode dives deep into the analysis of key characters, their stories, and the traumas they reflect within five categories. We focus on Possessed, Vengeful, Grief-stricken, Hysterical, and Objectified. By exploring these portrayals, the podcast aims to shed light on how horror films mirror real-life fears and societal anxieties through their female characters. Keep up with the news at www.momoshaty. com.

EXQUISITE CORPSE

This is not a dog

Invented by surrealists, an exquisite corpse is a game in which writers collaborate to create a story, but each author contributes knowing only the passage that came directly before them. Over 100 writers participated in our contest, each competing against at least ten others to write the best continuation of the previous scene. This is how their story unfolded.

YOU SEE A DOG at the end of an alleyway, and something unusual comes out of its mouth.

THE MAN AT THE 7-ELEVEN COMPLAINS THAT YOU'RE HOLDING UP THE LINE as you pry open the eye drops you just bought. You blink medicated saline tears down both cheeks, and promptly jog back across the street to the alleyway. Back to the collie.

The dog is still there. Still without an owner. Still without a collar. Still placidly staring at you. You chuckle, relieved that it had just been the spring pollen playing itchy tricks on your vision, but then the dog's mouth slowly unhinges a second time. Your breath hitches in your throat as a sea of action figure sized humanoid arms once again begin swaying and undulating from within its maw, like hungry baby birds awaiting a meal. Panic floods you as the tiny arms work together, twisting and posing to re-form the ominous word that had first sent you running to the convenience store. SOON.

By MICHAEL BOULERICE

YOUR INSTINCTS SCREAM AT YOU to run away from the dog's ominous warning. But your memories override them. It looks like your grandfather's collie, who led lambs from danger and once dragged you to shelter during a storm. The humanoid arms protruding from its mouth are not so strange. You once pulled the limbs off your boyhood action figures, examining their superhero physiques, testing whether their bulging muscles would bounce back when you squashed them in the vice in your father's workshop.

"Hey boy!" you say, reaching out to stroke the dog. It grins then turns away. You follow, running carefree along the dark alley, the warning forgotten, until you reach an open square carpeted with plastic dolls. Their limbless torsos writhe painfully. Their pink mouths are screaming soundlessly. The dog turns to face you. The tiny arms in its mouth twist and pose to form the word NOW.

By ALEX GREHY

THE DOG'S EYES SHIMMER with wetness. Thick black streaks running down its snout. The disarming word sags from the dog's mouth until it's indecipherable; a lolling pink fiber unfurling, slipping into a puddle of stale rainwater. The dog sputters and retches. Coughs up the last bit. You cover your mouth against the stench. Sour rotting garlic. You think of your grandfather in those final days, laying in his own filth. His clouding eyes pleading. His lips cracked and parting. NOW.

You wait a moment, expecting the dog to lap up its own sickness. The poor thing whines and pads further into the alley. You step forward and reach down. Thrust your hand into the soft mess. Grasping fingers slick with bile. Until you find it.

By MAV LUX

EVEN AS YOU'RE CLEANING OFF THE SICK, the pulse gives it away. The heart is warm. Beating. Tattered arteries still attached; the surface covered with so much fat it's more white than red. In the distance, the same dog whimpers in rhythm until the beat swells and is all you hear. *Lub-dub, lub-dub, lub-dub* but to you it sounds like *eat me,* and you can't think why not.

Despite the scent of copper and dog-breath, you don't resist the compulsion to bite. Your mouth opens and chews, slurps the arteries like spaghetti. The raw muscle so tough your jaw throbs as the last chunks slide down your throat and land like a stone in the pit of your stomach. As if you've swallowed it whole. There's no one to ask whose life you've consumed or whose heart will be next.

By YELENA CRANE

BUT THERE NEVER TRULY WAS A QUESTION AS TO WHO WOULD BE NEXT, is there? Because your thoughts are becoming less and less important. No longer fueled by logic. Feeling. You're succumbing to base instincts. Primal urges. Your brain has been transformed by the strange and gory feast you've participated in.

Viscera hangs from your lips, gristle stuck between your teeth as you catch a familiar scent in the air — stale cigarettes cut by floral perfume — guiding you toward your next victim. The distant thrum of their heart beats in a subtle arrhythmia you've heard countless times, your ear pressed to their chest. No longer a comfort, but a craving.

By MICHAEL BETTENDORF

YOU WILL NEVER FORGET THAT CLOYING SCENT, sticking against the insides of your nostrils, like it never left. *Ma.* Before you realize it, you're there, at her grave, granules of moist dirt wedging themselves under each fingernail. It doesn't make any sense, her having died years ago, but that heartbeat cannot be ignored. You want her now; you want that leathery skin, those raspy lungs.

Six feet down now and all that's left until you have Ma again is some rotting wood. Your skin rips, shreds, disintegrates as you reach through what's left of her coffin. You need it, you need *her,* but what you have in your hands now isn't Ma. It's that dog, the one from earlier, but desiccated now, its maw still hung open, its deep black eyes still glaring at you with that menacing scowl.

By RYAN MARIE KETTERER

FROM THE DEAD DOG'S BLACK THROAT SPILLS the tender scent of her. Rotting ribs press in as you hold her too close, as a child would, sloughing off her rotted pelt in great sloppy sheafs. The skin swaddles you. Warm, viscous liquid slides down your leg. Ma takes you into her cavernous maw, swallowing you down a tunnel of muscle until you're clutched in her stomach like an embrace. You curl up in pain, free-floating in gastric acid that must be made of that scent, that scent, sticking to your skin like boiling oil. It's the kind of agony Catholics dream of. Then the whole stomach, small around you as a coffin, spasms and spasms until you're vomited up head-first.

You emerge from rotted, canine teeth. Oh god. It was you. It was *you*.

By ARCHER GRID

YOU HAVE FOUND A MIRROR IN A FESTERING DOG because once you turn, once you look back, it's so clear. You're expecting Ma, a decaying home, but the only canines in this grave dangle from decomposing human gums by chewy threads of root. Those too-sharp teeth had the other eighth-graders asking if your juicebox was full of blood. Of course these are your teeth, in your skinless head, on what's left of your body.

Gastric acid fumes off your skin as you stare. In your grave, the you that is not you blinks parasite-pocked eyes. Its chest is a caved-in stock pot, blood bubbling up and over. You exhale, and the thoracic volcano forms a bloody bubble that grows, stretches, covers your corpse until the red sheen is a dome between you and it. Your fingers ache. You need to find out what else will pop if this does.

By ELIS MONTGOMERY

YOU PUSH, interlaced fingers pressed together, forming a tapered point, a spear to thrust into the membrane. The surface trembles, flexing under your fingertips, spasming under the bloody blistered film. Your probing finds a weakness — a point of entry, and it splits open to admit your hands with a liquid slap, a gush of released pressure, and a thick spray of hot, noisome slime.

The oozing filth, gray in the thin light, envelops your arms as they sink in, elbow deep. The meaty scent of afterbirth chokes your ravaged throat, but there is something primal in the tang, an urging recollection, of being nursed at Ma's breast. Something solid brushes your hands and there's a noise, more felt than heard; a drowned, mewling, animalistic sound. So you tear at the rupture, ripping ribbons out of the dreadful corpse-womb to draw its occupant into the light.

By STEVEN PATCHETT

BATHED IN THE DIM GLOW, IT CRIES, hacking amniotic juices from its dripping maw. Its heft spills from the steaming corpse onto the ground before you. Thin legs twitch beneath the remnants of a milky sac. Gingerly, you pluck away the shreds, exposing the squirming beast.

You lean back, lap at the sweat dripping from your crown, and take in the bleating innocence. A desperate hatchling, its mother little more than meat to fester. You look toward the gaping cavern and feel its honeyed beckon. This will not do, you decide, shifting closer. Your sticky hands plunge in again. They pull away plump, shiny inners. You sing lullabies as you work, comforting your newfound babe. It fits exquisitely when it is ready. Your limbs stretch beneath their new skin, your claws spread and tap at asphalt. The infant stumbles toward you, and you lap at its temple. Together, you go.

By XOCHILT AVILA

Exquisite Corpse contributors

Michael Boulerice (he/him) hails from the wilds of New Hampshire. His stories can be found with Tenebrous Press, Cosmic Horror Monthly, *the* Creepy Podcast, *and many other outlets. When he's not pouring the unfortunate contents of his brain into a keyboard, Michael is either snowboarding in the White Mountains, or spoiling his pets rotten.*

Alex Grehy's ingredients for contentment are her rescue greyhounds, singing, chocolate, and exploring England's canals in her narrowboat — it's a sweet life. Living in light enables her to see the shadows in which the elements of horror lurk. Alex (she/her) is inspired by the natural world around her, her imagination making unique connections expressed in vivid prose and thought-provoking poetry. Her poetry collection, Last Species Standing *(Alien Buddha Press/Amazon) is a captivating exploration of the intricate relationship between humanity, nature and the ever-evolving realm of technology.*

Mav lives and writes in the desert with his family and small army of cats. He can usually be found dreaming of rain while watching horror films.

Yelena Crane is a Ukrainian/Soviet born and USA based writer, incorporating a mix of borscht to burgers influences into her work. With an advanced degree in the sciences, she has followed her passions from mad scientist to sci-fi writer. Her stories often explore the boundaries of technology, the complexities of human nature, and the consequences of our choices. She's published in Nature Futures, Dark Matter, Flame Tree, Third Flatiron, *and elsewhere. Follow her @Aelintari, yelenacrane.bsky.social, and https:// www.yelenacrane.com.*

Michael Bettendorf (he/him) is a writer from the Midwest who's glad his dog is not like the one in this story. His debut experimental gamebook, Trve Cvlt, *is out now at Tenebrous Press. You can find links to his writing at www.michaelbettendorfwrites.com.*

Ryan Marie Ketterer is an author and editor from Malden, Massachusetts. Her editorial debut, Welcome to Your Body: Lessons in Evisceration, *released in May 2024 from Salt Heart Press. Her short fiction can be found in* Clarkesworld, Cosmic Horror Monthly, *and various anthologies. She's a fan of the weird and uncanny, and when she isn't writing or editing, you can find her coding or off in the woods. She's on Twitter and Instagram at @ RyanMarie47.*

Archer Grid. reader. writer. lady-liker. Support Women's Wrongs - *Read my Sapphic Heist Romance,* GIRL WITH NO NAME, *at ARCHERGRID.SUBSTACK.COM. Socials: @archergrid.*

Elis Montgomery is a speculative fiction writer from Vancouver, Canada. She is a member of SFWA and Codex. When she's not writing, she's usually hanging upside down in an aerial arts class or a murky cave. Find her there or at elismontgomery. com. If you have anything to spare, please consider donating to Palestinian children in need of medical care in Gaza: https://pcrf1.app.neoncrm.com/forms/ gaza-recovery.

Steven Patchett is an Engineer, Father and Writer in the North East of England. He's been published here and there, and can be found on Twitter and Bluesky, being encouraging. @StevenPatchett7 & @ stevenpatchett.bsky.social.

Xochilt Avila (they/them) is a queer horror author in Maryland, USA. Their experience living outside of binary labels has fostered their passion for justice, horror, and all things "strange." You can find updates on their work on Twitter @XAvilaWrites and reach them at xochiltavilabooks@gmail.com. If you're able, they ask that you consider donating to Palestinian aid, such as to the Palestine Children's Relief Fund at pcrf.net.

CLASSIFIEDS

Connections from across the world—find goods, services, noble causes, and screams in the void here.

SHELTER FOR OUR FRIENDS
Looking for a cat or dog near Huntley, IL? Adopt, don't shop! Animal House Shelter is looking for responsible parents and donations. To visit or donate, start at animalhouseshelter.com.

STAPLED SPINE / STAPLED SOUNDS
A physical horror fanzine and a weekly radio show streaming everywhere! 90's technology TODAY! Entertaining Horror fans one black-clad galoot at a time! Linktr.ee/StapledSpine.

WITH LOVE AND SORROW
In loving memory of Eirik Gumeny, who wrote with wit and humor, edited with passion and integrity, and cared with his whole heart. His loss is so deeply felt among his peers and loved ones. If you haven't yet, meet him by reading his *Exponential Apocalypse* series, or "the book of

(his) heart (and diseased lungs)", *Infernal Organs.*

"'Yes' and 'no' feel heavy, harsh. But 'maybe' is kind of like looking up at the endless night sky."

— Eirik Gumeny

DONATE TO COTA.ORG
COTA can help remove the financial barriers to a life-saving transplant by providing fundraising assistance and family support.

SPLURGE ON CREATIVITY
Hand sewn blank journals with parchment interiors and hand made Lokta paper covers. SPECIAL: 10 journals for $35. The perfect gifts for the holidays. moranpress.com.

BRAIN ~~SWAP~~ WANTED
~~TRADES ONLY. Mine's out, in fishbowl. It's clean, fish was flushed. NO SCAMMERS! NO LOWBALL OFFERS! I know what I got here!~~ Good news! Fish is fine. Cash in hand.

CURSED DRUMHEAD GIVEAWAY
Walls as blank as your soul? Spruce them up with a custom drumhead. Tag @BeardedBetts on X with your TRVest story, TRVest underrated band, or corpse paint selfie. Selfies worth x10 entries.

BE THE STORY
Embark on a haunted house journey where you're the main character. Lonely House is a hybrid horror novella and solo role-playing game narrated by Rain Corbyn. On Audible: audible.com/pd/Lonely-House-Audiobook/B0CLT81V98.

EYE-CATCHING HORROR BOOKS
Looking for more diverse indie horror and dark fantasy? With an ever-growing roster of talented new authors, Ghost Orchid Press has you covered! Visit us today for all your dark fiction needs. linktr.ee/ghostorchidpress.

LF CYBERPUNK CLOWN FANS
If you're intrigued at the prospect of cyberpunk masochist clowns, do read Sara S. Messenger's short story "The Clown Watches the Clown" published this year in Apex Magazine Issue 144!

WE BLEED ORANGE & BLACK
The podcast for Halloween & Horror lovers! Join us as we interview creators, discuss our favorite horror and share original scary stories. webobpodcast. com @webobpcast iTunes – Spotify.

NO MIND LEFT BEHIND
Mind (UK) & Mental Health America are here to listen. I was an angry and frustrated ten-year-old. Mind taught me to focus on creative outlets for my rage. No one should struggle alone. mind.org.uk/donate; mhanational.org/donate.

THE MALARKER
Sign up for our newsletter. Stories, updates, and discounts in your inbox. No paywall. Best way to keep up with Malarkey Press news because who knows when Twitter will die or lock us out. malarkeyforall.substack.com.

HAZEL ZORN: ILLUSTRATOR
Blackwork illustrations of nature or horror subjects. Consult fee and completed piece price range $70-$150 hazelzorn@gmail.com/ IG: hazel.zorn.

COMICS IN NORTH PORTLAND!
Come visit Comic Cave PDX in the Kenton neighborhood of Portland, Oregon! A family-owned shop in a historic neighborhood with a nice variety of kid stuff, newsstand comics, and horror offerings. comiccavepdx.com.

FANCY A PLAY?
The Henriad by William Shakespeare. Fathers and sons. Kings and clowns. Battles and brothels. Shakespeare's epic trilogy about the rise of England's greatest king. Presented by Salt and Sage. Saltandsagepdx.org.

HPL FILM FESTIVAL
The only film festival that understands. Missed this year's programming? Not to worry, we stream it too! Subscribe for announcements: hplff.com/pdx.

SMALL DOG LF COMPANION
Mischevious mutt seeks bookish barker to be her begrudging adventure buddy. Must be small enough to curl up in a sock together. I promise to bamboozle only a little.

Want your own ad?

Letters to *The Skull & Laurel*

We want to start a dialogue on the stories featured in each issue of *The Skull & Laurel*, but we need your help. If you have any questions, concerns, criticism, or literary rants, we want to hear them! Email us at tenebrouspress.mag@gmail.com with the word "Letter" in the subject line, and you might just see your letter in a future issue.

CONTENT WARNINGS

Being a work of mature fiction, a degree of violence, gore, sex and/or death is to be expected in the stories contained in *The Skull & Laurel*.

For more specific concerns, please check the list of stories below for specific content warnings:

The Blind Cannot Judge Me, For They Cannot See I'm Good Inside:
systemic ableism, especially against the blind and neurodivergent; disabling as state oppression; forced monstrous pregnancy; drowning; violence against animals; thalassophobia; ecological collapse; cults; fascism

The Sea-Hare
gun violence

Dermatillomania
unchecked and severe symptons of anxiety, self-mutilation, body horror

CARTESIANA
death, bullying, child physical abuse

If We've Never Been Gone
animal death (hunting)

Dose of Dread: Never Waste a Drop
cannibalism

The Halved World
body horror, physical abuse

Variations on the Memory Palace:
abuse, loss of autonomy, cancer

Exquisite Corpse: This is not a dog
implied animal harm (not actually an animal)

Please be advised. More information at www.tenebrouspress.com.

Feeling weird?

READ WEIRD!

Grab your next
Tenebrous title.

Printed in the USA
CPSIA information can be obtained
at www.ICGtesting.com
LVHW061037060924
789772LV00002B/13

9 781959 790273